T0329212

Flirting with the enemy . . .

Ewan smiled. "Would you care to leave?"

Jo hesitated. "Where to?"

"Are you hungry?" he asked, a mischievous glint in his eye.

"Ravenous," she replied. What better place to pick Ewan's brain than at an intimate dinner for two?

"I don't feel like dealing with any crowds right now," he explained. "We could swing by my apartment and order in. That way we can really talk."

Uh-oh.

His apartment?

Jo didn't know what to say. Things were moving awfully fast. If Jo had been on a real first date—and not a secret mission—she would *never* go back to a guy's apartment. It was the baddest of all bad ideas.

Or was it?

She fingered the pea-size lump in the lining of her purse—the phone bug that she didn't get to install in Ewan's office that afternoon. Maybe she could get his home phone. . . .

With a sultry smile she slipped her hand into the crook of his elbow. "Ewan, I thought you'd never ask."

Don't miss any books in this thrilling new series:

Available from ARCHWAY Paperbacks

Spy Girls™

Live
and
Let Spy

by
Elizabeth Cage

AN ARCHWAY PAPERBACK
Published by POCKET BOOKS
New York   London   Toronto   Sydney   Tokyo   Singapore

AN ARCHWAY PAPERBACK *Original*

An Archway Paperback published by
POCKET BOOKS, a division of Simon & Schuster Inc.
1230 Avenue of the Americas, New York, NY 10020

Spy Girls™ is a trademark of Daniel Weiss Associates, Inc.

Produced by 17th Street Productions, a division of
Daniel Weiss Associates, Inc., New York

ISBN: 978-1-4814-2079-2

First Archway Paperback printing December 1998

10 9 8 7 6 5 4 3 2 1

To Laura Burns
and Michael Zimmerman,
les *cool cats* extraordinaires

Special thanks to Michael Zimmerman for his
assistance in the preparation of Live and Let Spy.

Live
and
Let Spy

Holy cow!" Theresa Hearth said as she checked out the spread of Godiva and strawberries on the huge conference table before her. "This is a diabetic's worst nightmare."

Caylin Pike grinned. "That which does not kill you will only make you fatter." She popped a plump strawberry into her mouth for emphasis.

"Like *you* have to worry about getting fat," Theresa muttered. "Run any marathons this morning?"

Caylin flipped her blond ponytail behind her and fired a roundhouse kick into the air. "Just a ten-K. But I *did* foil a few muggings on the way home."

"The world should know better than to mess with you, right?" Jo Carreras added, her dark eyes sparkling.

"Right." Caylin straightened her sweatshirt and gracefully slid into one of the massive conference room chairs. Her every move was lithe and athletic. "So what's the deal with this room? It's big enough for a game of racquetball. And it looks so . . . *sterile.*"

"No kidding," Theresa replied, scanning the

high white walls and hidden fluorescent lights. The chamber had to be at least a hundred feet long and thirty feet wide. The only furnishings were the gigantic white conference table and three expensive-looking white leather chairs.

One chair for each of the Spy Girls.

"Sometimes The Tower really creeps me out," Theresa remarked. She ran a hand nervously through her tousled brown hair. "It's like they plan everything with only us in mind."

"Like they know what we're thinking at all times," Jo agreed. She approached one of the empty chairs tentatively, then tippy-tapped away in her Manolo Blahnik mules.

"Sit down, you guys," Caylin said impatiently. "I bet the show's not going to start until we're all in our seats."

Theresa and Jo remained rooted to the glossy, futuristic hospital-white floor.

Caylin's blue eyes widened indignantly. "What, do you think the chairs will flip over backward and set you on fire like in *Austin Powers?*"

Theresa laughed. "I loved that part."

"Hey, *not* funny," Jo pleaded. "There's something about this room that . . . I don't know. It's *freaky.*"

"Look, The Tower handpicked us to save the world, remember?" Caylin said. "We're the good guys. Nothing bad's going to happen to us here."

Theresa snagged a piece of chocolate and

slowly sat down. The chair was surprisingly soft and comfortable. No fire, no flipping. "You know, Jo *does* have a point," she began. "This is the kind of room where presidents decide which countries to bomb. We trained in this building for four months and we didn't even know this room *existed.* Good guys or not, doesn't that weird you out in the slightest?"

"Nope," Caylin replied, popping another juicy berry.

"Whoa! Careful with that juice, Cay," Jo warned as she sat down gingerly in the last remaining empty chair. "Would you like the honor of paying my next dry-cleaning bill?"

Caylin pretended to lob a chocolate in Jo's direction. "What do you care when The Tower's picking up the tab?"

"Oh yeah . . . you're right." Jo smoothed her pristine Prada pencil skirt over her knees. "So why did we get summoned here, anyway?"

Caylin sipped from a bottle of water. "I guess we've got another secret mission ahead of us."

"But we only got back from England forty-eight hours ago," Theresa moaned.

"Yeah," Jo chimed in. "That's not even enough time to go *shopping,* let alone celebrate our first victorious mission."

Caylin grinned. "We *did* kick butt."

"You expected anything less?" Jo declared, reaching across the table and high-fiving her comrades. "The Spy Girls rule!"

"Well, we've only had one mission," Theresa said cautiously. "We're no Jane Bonds yet."

"*I* sure think we are," Caylin insisted. "Boy, T., you need to get your nose out of your laptop and take a good look around you. We totally saved the world last week. Didn't you notice?"

"Yeah." Theresa chuckled. "But didn't *you* notice how we almost got completely killed in the process? Hmmm . . . maybe all that bungee jumping has rattled your brain."

"And all that hacking has fried yours," Caylin said, giggling.

Theresa stuck out her tongue. "You couldn't hack your way out of a dressing room."

"Look, all joking aside," Jo interrupted with a smile, "don't forget that that's the whole point."

Theresa lifted an eyebrow. "What do you mean?"

"I mean, Caylin doesn't have to hack her way out of a dressing room because *you* can. Just like you don't have to bungee jump off Hoover Dam because Caylin can. We're all here because our skills complement each other, you know?"

Theresa gave Caylin a knowing look. "Hmmm . . . Jo must have been taking notes during our orientation speech."

"Naw, Jo was just paying extra-special attention to that speechifying hottie," Caylin quipped.

"So," Theresa mused, "if I'm Henrietta Hacker and Caylin is Action Jackson, then what does that make *you*, Jo?"

Jo half closed her eyelids. "I'm the seductress."

4

Theresa and Caylin groaned and pelted Jo with strawberries.

"My *skirt!*" Jo yelped. "Hey, watch the couture, okay?"

Their giggling stopped when the lights suddenly went dim. That could mean only one thing.

"Uncle Sam, is that you?" Theresa asked.

A low, powerful hum grew all around them. The Spy Girls glanced nervously at one another. The sound was everywhere, as if it came from deep within The Tower itself.

Slowly, on the far wall, a panel slid open and a giant screen appeared.

It glowed eerily. Blank.

"Time for *Captain Kangaroo*?" Jo whispered.

"Shhh," Theresa warned. Her heart pounded. She watched, hypnotized with curiosity, as The Tower's fearless leader, Uncle Sam, appeared on-screen. Fearless—and *faceless*. His image was digitally altered, pixilated like a surprise witness's on *Court TV*. These tiny electronic dots mixed with black, murky shadows to create an image that was more Grim Reaper than Guy Smiley.

"Welcome home, ladies," Uncle Sam said, his honey-rich voice full of pride. "And how are my favorite international spies doing today?"

"Ab fab," Jo said with a purr in her voice. "But we had *no* idea how terribly boring London could be this time of year, *dahling*. Was it the off-season for intrigue?"

"Hmmm, I believe it was," Caylin chimed in, employing her impeccable British accent. "*Do* send us somewhere a trifle more challenging this time, Samuel. I'm *dying* to know what's next."

"Don't die just yet, Caylin," Uncle Sam said ominously. "There'll be plenty of time for that later."

The girls glanced nervously at one another. Theresa gulped. Was good old Uncle Sammy *serious?*

The big screen was filled with the image of a sprawling, high-tech building. "This is the U.S. headquarters of InterCorp," Uncle Sam stated. "A multinational corporation that has reportedly been behind some of the more unsavory ventures in recent history. Toxic waste dumping, chemical weapons manufacturing, industrial espionage, you name it. Although we've kept the company under surveillance for years, no one has been able to dig up enough dirt to shut them down."

"I read an article about this company," Theresa said. "Supposedly key people who work for their competitors have a tendency to 'disappear.'"

"Supposedly," Jo spat. "Yeah, right."

The other girls knew not to comment when Jo used that tone of voice. That tone meant she was thinking of her father, a Miami judge who was gunned down right before the fourteen-year-old eyes of Josefina Mercedes Carreras while trying to convict a drug lord. Four years had passed since, but time had done little to soften the blow. Sure, Jo could easily hide her pain behind her naturally fun and flirty facade. But mentions of murder usually sent her crashing and burning.

"Like most people who run an empire with this much money and power, they want only one thing: more," Uncle Sam continued. "And they'll do *anything* to get it."

"Real sweethearts," Theresa said glibly, rolling her eyes.

A picture of an older, distinguished-looking man filled the screen. "This is Mitchell von Strauss, president of InterCorp," Uncle Sam said. "One of the most intelligent—and ruthless—businessmen in the world. His accomplishments speak for themselves. Unfortunately his methods do, too. He *eliminates* his competition—some say literally. One magazine compared him to a dangerous dictator— someone who thinks he can use any means to achieve his goals. Even murder."

"Disgusting," Jo said. Her dark eyes shot daggers at the image of von Strauss. Suddenly a new image appeared on-screen.

Jo's eyes instantly melted as she took in the vision of a tall, blond hottie with a deep tan and deeper dimples.

Ooh-la-la!

The one thing that could send Jo's caution, judgment, and common sense flying right out the window.

Ding!

"This is Ewan Gallagher, InterCorp's head of international relations," Uncle Sam explained.

"Relations?" Jo echoed. "Mmm. *I* can relate."

"He was a boy genius," Uncle Sam continued. "Graduated high school at fourteen, top of his class at Harvard at seventeen. Now, at just twenty-four, he's one of the most powerful men in international business."

Jo was practically drooling on the table.

"Wow," Caylin whispered. She looked as if she would hyperventilate at any second.

It wasn't like Caylin to be out of breath. But Jo sure couldn't blame her.

"Come on, you guys," Theresa muttered. "Can't you tell he's a guy who'd sell his mother on the black market?"

"So?" Jo replied dreamily.

"So, do you remember Antonio? The guy you hooked up with in London?" Theresa said. "Italian. Gorgeous. Charming. Liked to kill young female spies."

Jo scowled. "I remember."

"Theresa's right, girls," Uncle Sam said. "Don't judge this movie by its trailer. Gallagher is just as cold and ruthless as von Strauss."

Pouting, Jo tapped her high heels against the floor in frustration. She knew all too well how deceptive appearances could be—she'd had plenty of experience in that department. Still, for some bizarre reason she couldn't stop falling for dangerous guys. When she gazed up at Ewan's face on the screen, she didn't see cold and ruthless—just warm and guileless.

Note to self, she thought grimly. Get a clue!

She actually breathed a sigh of relief when a

gray, sleek-looking building replaced Ewan's face on the screen.

"This is InterCorp's Prague headquarters," Uncle Sam continued. "Von Strauss and Gallagher relocated to the Czech Republic's capital city just last week, presumably because an open-trade pact is about to be signed here."

"I love Prague!" Caylin said, ever the jet-setter. "It's so gorgeous."

"The New Russian Ballet likes Prague, too," Uncle Sam stated as footage of a gorgeous, dark-haired ballerina rolled. "This is Anka Perdova, age eighteen. She's the NRB's prima ballerina. The troupe is currently installed at Prague's St. Nikolai Theater."

"That's one big-buck investment," Caylin noted.

"Yes," Uncle Sam agreed. "And guess who is bankrolling their season in Prague?"

"InterCorp," Theresa replied.

"Exactly," Uncle Sam said.

"Why would InterCorp fund a ballet troupe?" Theresa asked.

"A tax write-off, probably," Uncle Sam replied. "And a smoke screen for their more devious doings."

Suddenly pictures of distinguished-looking men and women of all nationalities were flashing on the screen, rapid-fire. "In just eight days these dignitaries will be flooding Prague to finalize the aforementioned open-trade pact," Uncle Sam said. "It's scheduled to be signed immediately following a performance at the ballet."

"Let me guess," Jo said. "Something's going to go down during the performance."

"I'm getting to that," Uncle Sam said as a close-up picture of an older, graying gentleman filled the screen.

"He looks familiar," Caylin said.

"This is Gogol Karkovic, the prime minister of Varokhastan—a small, newly democratic Eastern European country," Uncle Sam explained. "If he signs the pact, InterCorp stands to lose a fortune."

"Why?" Theresa asked.

"Varokhastan is rich with mines," Uncle Sam replied. "*Diamond* mines. InterCorp has a vested interest in the diamond industry—and they're very possessive. They would like nothing more than to lay claim to the diamonds of Varokhastan. And as I mentioned before, they do *not* like competition—something this open-trade pact would create."

A million glittering diamonds filled the screen.

"Heaven," Jo said in awe.

"Not really," Uncle Sam said gravely. "We believe an attempt is going to be made on Karkovic's life before the trade pact can be signed. And we believe InterCorp is behind this assassination plot."

Jo gasped. An assassination plot? She instantly regretted her last breezy comment as images of her father flickered before her eyes.

"How will they do it?" Theresa asked, concern etched on her face.

Live and Let Spy

"That's for you to find out, Spy Girls," Uncle Sam replied.

"And for us to stop," Caylin added. She pounded a fist into her hand for emphasis.

"Exactly." Uncle Sam cleared his throat. "Don't forget who you're dealing with here. Men like von Strauss and Gallagher don't care who they destroy in their wake as long as they get what they're after."

"And that doesn't just mean Karkovic, right?" Theresa asked.

"You're right," Uncle Sam replied. Suddenly the image of Anka Perdova reappeared on-screen. This time she was smiling and signing autographs for a bunch of kids. "Who knows how far InterCorp's plans reach? They could endanger the whole ballet troupe. Everyone in the audience that night. The entire city of Prague. Young children, like the ones you see here. Karkovic may be their target, but anyone anywhere near the theater will be in danger—unless you foil InterCorp's plans."

Jo's eyes teared up at the poignant image. To think that such an awful thing could take place during a ballet performance—it seemed impossible.

As Jo watched the talented ballerina smile for the young children her heart leaped into her throat. She and Anka, on the surface, seemed so alike. They both had long black hair; they both were eighteen; heck, they both were even lefties. And now they were both wrapped up in a horrible assassination plot.

11

"Karkovic's bodyguards won't have a chance," Theresa stated.

"So what's the plan?" Caylin asked, bouncing up and down in her seat. Ready to run, move, do something, *anything*.

Uncle Sam exhaled deeply. "Girls, your mission is to infiltrate the open-trade conference and stop the assassination of Karkovic."

Theresa raised her hand as if she were in grade school. "Uh, we *knew* that already, Sam," she said half sarcastically. "Don't you have any more for us to go on?"

"Negative," Uncle Sam replied. "You're entirely on your own."

Caylin's brow furrowed. "Why us?" she asked. "This is a big challenge. I mean, we're talking global impact and stuff. Why don't you just notify the pros and let them handle it?"

"You *are* the pros," Uncle Sam responded testily. "Besides, it's all speculation at this point. The exposure of a formal investigation can't be risked. And since most of the stagehands and interns are young females, we thought you would arouse the least amount of suspicion. Feel up to it?"

"Do we have a *choice?*" Theresa scoffed. But her gray eyes were dancing with excitement.

A slow, sly grin grew across Caylin's face. "Well, I *do* love the ballet," she drawled. "And I've got *nothing* else on my schedule this week. I guess I can cope."

"Me too." Jo sighed dramatically. "So many evil schemes, so little time."

Uncle Sam chuckled. "Glad you're so confident, girls."

Theresa smiled. "Why's that, Sammy?"

"Because you ship out in two hours."

So is Prague gonna be cold or what?" Theresa asked as she stood in front of her walk-in closet. The Tower dorm room she shared with Theresa and Caylin was a blur of flying shirts, pants, and dresses as the trio attempted to get appropriately attired for the long plane ride ahead.

"*Freezing,*" Caylin said with a frown. "Which wouldn't be so bad if there were any mountains to snowboard. But Prague's not exactly the ski capital of the world."

"Too bad," Jo kidded, bundling socks. "You'll just have to concentrate on the silly old mission, won't you?"

"Drag," Caylin replied with a smirk. "I hate when that happens."

Theresa unplugged her laptop and slid it into its padded case. Sunlight streamed through the massive windows—warmth she wouldn't be seeing for a while. She selected the CD remote from the eight remotes on her night table and aimed it at the far wall. "I can't even hear myself think."

Miles Davis faded slightly. Theresa chose another remote and switched the channel from

MTV to CNN, hoping to catch a glimpse of a global weather report.

"I'm going to miss this entertainment center." Theresa sighed. "CD, VHS, DVD, HDTV, N64. We've got it all, but we only had two days to enjoy it."

"That's because you just had to rewire the whole wall before we left for London," Caylin said. "You're the only one who knows how to work everything. I mean, we have eight remotes!"

"They're labeled," Theresa explained.

"I still can't tell them apart." Caylin stared longingly at her snowboard, which she had mounted on the wall above her bed. "I just wish I could bring my board. What a bummer."

"I can't say I'm looking forward to icicles, either," Jo went on, folding a sweater. "After all, this bod's too dope to hide in a coat!"

Theresa giggled. "We're going on a *mission*, Jo. Not a vacation."

"A mission that we have *no time* to pack for," Caylin interjected. "What kind of wardrobe can a girl pack in no time?"

"Sometimes you guys amaze me." Theresa sighed. "A prominent world leader is about to be assassinated, and you two are worried about clothes."

Theresa gestured toward the giant TV screen. There Gogol Karkovic was being shown meeting young children who had been orphaned during the course of a recent civil war. Tears shone in the older man's eyes as he spoke in his native Varok.

Live and Let Spy

The caption at the bottom of the screen read, *We cannot live in a world where guns make the law— where children are left to suffer alone.*

The room fell silent as Theresa clicked off the remote.

Jo squinted. Karkovic's message had clearly hit home with her. "Well, come on, we *do* have to wear *something*," she began, ignoring the heartwrenching newscast. "Some help you are, Theresa. I still can't believe your mother is a fashion designer."

Theresa rolled her eyes. "I know, I know."

"I really *don't* get it, T." Caylin shook her head sadly. "How can you hate fashion when we have The Tower buying us clothes? You could get couture for the asking, sweetie darling, but all you want to do is wear jeans."

"I have better things to worry about," Theresa muttered, arranging her laptop and an array of peripherals on the bed.

"You and your toys," Jo kidded. "I'm gonna call Danielle and see if she has any last minute advice for us."

She went to grab the proper remote, but she could only stare, dumbfounded, at the lineup of controllers on Theresa's night table.

"Okay, T.," Jo growled. "I give up. Which one works the TV phone?"

"Third from the left," Theresa replied without looking up from her hardware.

"I hate these things," Jo said. "Can't we just get one big remote?"

"It'd be the size of a mainframe," Theresa said with a laugh.

Jo sighed and punched in 03-14-83—the secret code to activate the TV phone and Taylor Hanson's birthday. "Oh, Danielle, are you home?" Jo asked as the big TV came back to life with a flashing blue screen and the word *ringing* emblazoned across it.

Theresa couldn't help but smile at the mention of Danielle's name. When they were in London, the Spy Girls had seen a tall woman with short brown hair following them everywhere. They had been certain that "Short Hair" was working for the enemy and had tried desperately to learn her identity by snapping her picture with their secret cameras and chasing her through nightclubs.

"Boy, did I feel stupid when we found out Danielle was actually one of us," Theresa said.

"I know," Jo replied, dropping the remote on the bed. "I about had a cow when we got to the safe house and *bam,* there she was."

Theresa immediately retrieved the remote from the bed and replaced it on her nightstand. "I'm glad we've got her on our side. We're sure going to need her help on this mission."

A few seconds later Danielle's face appeared on the big screen. "Hello, Spy Girls," she chirped. "Ready to roll?"

"Hardly." Theresa moaned, pointing to the T-shirt and boxers she was still lounging around in. "I'm so clueless about clothes, I can't even figure out what to wear on the plane."

"You better get a move on," Danielle instructed. "You have less than an hour."

"I know," Caylin said, running a brush through her long blond hair. "Any Prague pointers?"

"Just keep a cool head," Danielle instructed. "This is a high-pressure mission, seeing as the pact signing is just over a week away. Stay focused and take it one step at a time."

"As long as those one-steps-at-a-time bring down InterCorp, it'll be *all* good," Jo said enthusiastically.

Danielle smiled. "Now, when you land, you need to tell your driver to take you to Josefská two-four-two, three-S. Is someone writing this down?"

"I am," Theresa said, grabbing the nearest pen and paper. "So it's what?"

"*J-o-s-e-f-s-k-á* two-four-two, three-S," Danielle repeated. "Got it?"

"Yep," Theresa said, writing down the letters in a sure, block script.

"I'll be there in thirty minutes to take you to the airport," Danielle said. "Good luck, girls!"

The screen faded to black.

"Hope we don't need it," Theresa muttered.

"Five minutes late." Caylin scowled as she hopped around impatiently in the designated Tower pickup area. "Danielle is five minutes late. Where is she?"

Jo whipped out her cell phone. She was just about to dial Danielle's digits when she heard the sound of screeching tires.

19

Delicious. Jo loved that sound. She could practically smell the burning rubber already.

A sleek, lobster red blur roared around the corner, fishtailing and squealing to a halt in front of her.

Jo's tongue practically rolled out to the ground. There it sat, right in front of her. Jo Carreras's weakness number two—a gorgeous sports car. A brand-new Ferrari F50, to be exact, with Danielle grinning from the driver's seat.

"No way—an F-Fifty!" Jo gasped as she ran a hand over the sweet ride's shiny enamel. "Where'd you score this?"

"Didn't think I was this cool, did you?" Danielle opened the door and slid out. "This beauty was confiscated in a big drug bust a few weeks back. And when they plea-bargained the guy yesterday, the car stopped being evidence and started being mine. At least for a couple of days."

"You gotta let me drive, Danielle," Jo demanded, circling the vehicle like a lioness stalking her prey. *"Now."*

"No way." She shook her head. "The only one getting behind that wheel is me."

"Guess again, Sherlock." Jo swiped the keys from the ignition. "Formula One construction, nitrogen hydraulic suspension, ABS racing brakes— ohh, I *need* this."

"Say, Wonder Wheels," Theresa interrupted. "Where are *we* supposed to sit?"

"Yeah," Caylin agreed. "There're only two seats!"

Jo shrugged. "Cram in the back."

Live and Let Spy

"With our *bags?*" Theresa asked incredulously.

"Come on," Jo grumbled, flipping the driver's seat forward and stuffing her bag in the tiny space behind it.

As Caylin slid uncomfortably into the Ferrari she glared at Danielle. "Couldn't get a limo, huh?"

"Who needs a limo when you've got a Ferrari?" Jo breathed. "We'll be at the airport in seven minutes."

"*Seven?*" Theresa exclaimed, eyes wide.

"Okay, six."

"*Danielle,*" Theresa and Caylin complained in stereo.

"Don't worry," Danielle soothed. "I won't let Jo kill us."

Caylin and Theresa stuffed their bags—and each other—into the tiny space behind the two seats. Their heads were scrunched against the tan leather roof and their limbs tangled in their luggage.

"You do realize, Jo, that if we die now, no one will be left to save the world," Caylin stated dryly.

"Relax," Jo replied, smoothly slipping the car into gear. She revved the engine methodically. "With a V-twelve, four hundred horses, we'll go from zero to one-double-oh in three-point-seven seconds."

"Is that with or without the air bag?" Theresa asked.

Jo gave her a grin, pressed her pedal to the metal, and peeled out. "Prague, here we come!" she screamed.

"his is it." Theresa surveyed the homes along the winding cobblestone street. She scanned the piece of paper on which she had scrawled the address. "I think."

"After an hour in customs I can't keep anything straight," Caylin said crankily.

Jo squinted at a map. "Malá Strana," she recited, ever the language expert. "The Little Quarter district of Prague. Our new home."

"Mozart used to walk these streets all the time," Theresa revealed. "But I doubt he lived *here.*"

Theresa pointed at the door in front of her for emphasis. The number 242 was painted next to it haphazardly. Drop-jawed, she gazed up and up—the run-down building was five stories tall. Forbidding stone gargoyles stared down at her from the rooftop. "It looks so . . . old."

"Chances are, it is," Caylin quipped.

"Could this all be for us?" Jo whispered.

"*Not,*" Caylin said, dropping her bags by her feet. "It looks like my aunt's apartment building in Paris. Didn't Danielle give a flat number?"

Theresa squinted at the crumpled piece of paper. "Three-S."

"There you go, Watson," Caylin said, picking up her bags and jaunting toward the door with a new spring in her step. "What did you think the three-S stood for?"

"Three spies, of course," Theresa said. "Hey, who's got the key?"

Caylin produced the envelope that a stern flight attendant had slipped to her during the flight. Inside were two keys. Caylin unlocked the heavy, hand-carved door and pushed it open. "Okay—I bet three means third floor," Caylin said, heading for the steep stairwell before them.

"No elevator?" Jo whined, looking disdainfully at the water-stained walls and worn gray carpet covering the stairs. "This is a far cry from the Ritz."

Indeed, the worn-down carpet and water-stained walls looked positively dilapidated compared to the decadent digs they'd dwelled in just days earlier.

When they reached the third floor and laid eyes on the scratched-up door marked 3-S, their expectations deflated even further.

"This is a nightmare," Jo said, her nose wrinkled.

"You can say that again," Caylin agreed, turning the key in the lock. But when the door swung wide, she gasped. "Check it out!" she cheered, spinning around to soak in the red velvet couch, the ornate woodwork, the abstract art on the walls, the giant aquarium.

"Can you say *delish?*" Theresa exclaimed. She

slipped her sneakers off and ran her bare feet over the soft oriental rug. "The Tower has really outdone itself this time."

"Too cool!" Jo squealed, dumping her bags and dashing into a bedroom. "Whoa—a four-post canopy bed!" she hollered, prompting Theresa and Caylin to run in after her.

"Talk about perfect!" Theresa shrilled.

"Hurry up," Caylin prodded after scanning the room. "I want to see more!"

All the bedrooms had massive canopy beds and antique decor. The ceilings had to be fifteen feet high, with long windows framed by heavy red velvet drapes.

"Check out the new laptop in here," Caylin said, pointing into the middle bedroom. "Wow, a rolltop desk, a fax machine—man, this room is totally equipped!"

Theresa gasped. *"Mine!"* She marched in and dropped her bag by the bed, gazing lovingly at the setup before her. "Mine, mine, mine, mine, mine! Ooh, I've been *dying* to get my hands on one of these—a Powerbook Fourteen-hundred-c with a fifty-six-K internal modem!" Theresa plopped into the high-back wooden chair and punched away furiously at the keys. "Wow. A good computer can be so . . . *sexy.*"

Jo grabbed Theresa's arm and yanked her away from the laptop.

"Hey!"

"No net surfing till we see the rest of the

place!" Jo ordered. "Let's check out the living room."

"And the fridge!" Caylin added.

En route to the kitchen Theresa spied a note resting on the corner of the massive antique dining room table. "Uh-oh, gal pals," she exclaimed. "We have a love letter!"

As Theresa snatched up the paper Caylin and Jo dashed over at lightning speed.

"Push the red button on the aquarium," Theresa read, glancing up at Caylin and Jo with a quizzical look in her eyes.

"Go for it," Caylin instructed.

Theresa pressed the red button on top of the aquarium. Nothing happened.

"Press it again," Caylin said, reaching for it.

"No, wait," Theresa replied. "Look."

The long side of the aquarium actually flickered. Gradually Uncle Sam's shadowed face appeared in the glass.

"That's so cool!" Theresa exclaimed, meeting Jo's and Caylin's gazes. "You can still see the fish. Is this an LCD or what?"

"That's top secret, Theresa," Uncle Sam replied.

"No fair."

The Spy Girls plopped down on the expensive-looking chairs and couches around the living room.

"Time to get down to business, ladies," he said.

"Cool," Caylin replied. She scooted to the edge of her seat in delicious anticipation. "Let's have it."

"There are three computerized notebooks in

the drawer embedded in the base of the aquarium," Uncle Sam said. "Take notes."

Theresa ran over and retrieved the futuristic notepads—slim, miniaturized versions of a laptop—and passed them out to her eager counterparts. "Ready, Sammy," she said, placing her fingers on the keys expectantly.

"You're all to report for duty tomorrow—that's Monday morning—at ten A.M.," Uncle Sam instructed. "Jo, you'll pose as Selma Ribiero, a Brazilian-American daughter of wealthy parentage. You're interning at InterCorp so that you can learn the ins and outs of big business."

Jo grinned wickedly.

"Already dreaming about rubbing elbows with Ewan Gallagher?" Caylin teased.

"No," Jo said lightly. "Just dreaming about saving the world, that's all."

Caylin laughed. "I do that, too, but it doesn't make me blush."

"Let's move on," Uncle Sam admonished. "Theresa, you'll be posing as Tiffany Heileman, an American who's interning at the ballet in the props department."

"*Tiffany?*" Theresa scoffed. "Does a bleach job and frosted pink lip gloss come with that alias?"

Uncle Sam remained silent. While she couldn't see his face, Theresa could practically feel his glare.

"Sorry," she murmured. "Tiffany's . . . great. No complaints from me."

"Good." Uncle Sam cleared his throat. "Caylin, you're posing as Australian exchange student Muriel

Hewitt, who's ushering at the theater for some extra cash."

"All righty, mate!" she replied in her best Aussie accent. "If I can't surf down under, at least I can talk about it."

"The information on where to go and who to report to is in the locked safety-deposit box under the sink," Uncle Sam continued, "and the key is taped to a sour spot in the refrigerator."

"Sour spot?" Theresa repeated. "Let's see—sour cream, sour milk, sweet-and-sour sauce. . . ."

Uncle Sam chuckled. "Your wardrobes will be delivered shortly."

"Whoo-hoo!" Jo and Caylin cheered.

"But answer the door *only* to those who use the secret buzz."

The intercom suddenly buzzed. Two short, two long.

Caylin rolled her eyes.

"I saw that!" Uncle Sam said.

"Saw what?" Caylin asked innocently.

"The eye roll, that's what," he said, thankfully not sounding *too* mad. "You're on video cam, too."

"Really? Where is it?" Theresa said, looking up, down, and all around to track the location of the hidden lens.

"You tell me," he dared.

Theresa went to the aquarium and began to inspect it inch by inch. "Check it out!" she called. "One of those fish swimming behind Uncle Sam is actually a camera."

Live and Let Spy

"OK, Sam, you got me," Caylin said as she looked directly into the faux goldfish's mouth, where a camera lens was hidden. "But isn't a secret buzz a little much?"

"Not if the people on the other side of the door have guns," Uncle Sam said.

"Good point," Jo admitted.

"Good point indeed. And good night." Uncle Sam's shadowy image dissolved into the aquarium's crystal blue water.

"This is totally wild," Jo said.

"I'll say," Caylin agreed. "I've always wanted to be an Aussie!" She broke into her best Sydney accent. "Let's go suss out that sour spot."

Jo and Caylin ambushed the fridge while Theresa checked out the equipment.

"This kitchen is loaded," Theresa noted. "Fresh fruit, juice machine, espresso . . . why go out?"

"Where's that key . . . ," Caylin grumbled. "Lemonade?" She examined the ceramic pitcher for the magic key. "Nope, no cigar. Maybe pickles?"

"What about lemon balls?" Jo proposed, looking bored with the search. "Do they have those in Prague?"

Caylin unscrewed the lid of the pickle jar. "Bingo!" she cheered, snatching the key from inside the lid.

"Now that all the secret bells and whistles are out in the open," Jo said, "I'm going to unpack and unwind."

The others agreed. An hour later essentials

were stowed, snacks were scarfed, and the Spy Girls were ready to rock.

"Okay," Jo began as she dabbed pink polish on her toenails. "Here's a little vocab lesson. There are about a dozen ways to say 'cute' in Czech, but I'll give you three."

"How challenging," Caylin called out from the kitchen, where she was whipping up a goulash dinner to celebrate their first night in Prague. "Just don't quiz me later, okay?"

"One, there's *roztomily*, which is a charming kind of cute," Jo continued, unfazed. "Then there's *cimansky*, which is *cute*-cute—you know, like 'that little big-eyed puppy is totally *cimanzky*.' And then there's *mazany*, which is foxy . . . literally."

"Thanks, Jo," Theresa drawled. "I'm sure *that'll* come in handy the next time I'm in a bind."

Caylin jumped out of the kitchen. She clapped and rolled her eyes up melodramatically. "'Please, sir, don't kill me—I find you so . . . *mazany!*'" she cried breathily.

"I'm just going to stick to my pocket translator, thank you very much." Theresa waved the thin, checkbook-size computer in the air for emphasis.

"You guys just don't know how to have fun." Jo sighed as she finished up her pedicure. "You know, it's amazing how the right polish and a kickin' toe ring can make the ugliest part of the body look fabulous."

Theresa looked up from her laptop. "You know, what's *really* amazing is how much time people

30

spend painting their fingers and toes and faces. It just doesn't seem sensible."

"I think you've been surfing that web too long, my darling," Caylin called out. "Try some *real* surfing and you'll see the world in a whole different way."

"Sports and makeup." Theresa rolled her eyes. "Sorry, but I don't see the connection."

Buzz-buzz . . . buzzzzzzzz-buzzzzzzzz.

Jo jumped in surprise at the sound of the intercom. Thankfully her perfect polish remained intact.

"The secret buzz!" Theresa whispered.

"That's our wardrobe!" Jo exclaimed. She hobbled toward the door on her heels to avoid damaging her tantalizing tootsies. "Who *iiis* it?" she asked, peering through the peephole.

"Special delivery," the guy behind the door called.

Panting, she turned to Theresa and Caylin. "He's *foxy!*" Jo whispered.

"Don't you mean *mazany?*" Theresa and Caylin teased in stereo.

The "Mystery Date" song played in Jo's head as she opened the door, revealing a tall, muscular guy with long blond hair and a bright smile.

"I w-would like to, h-how you say, *greet* you," he mumbled in stilted English.

Jo held out her hand. "You mean, *hello.*"

The delivery guy ignored her hand and squinted at her. "Yes . . . hello. I have boxes."

He turned and began unloading cardboard boxes from his dolly. Each box was marked with one of their names. The muscles in his forearms rippled like steel cables.

Mmm, *yummy.*

Jo grinned at the others, wiggling her eyebrows. "Those boxes look heavy," she said to him.

He stared at her feet. "Pink."

She showed off her pearly pink toenails. "You like?"

He gave her a strange look and walked out.

"What's *his* damage?" Jo whispered to her compatriots. Still, she couldn't help admiring his fair form as he brought in the last box.

"I go now," he said.

"Wait!" Jo cried.

The guy froze.

"Jo, the gentleman should *go* now," Caylin explained politely.

"I *know*, Cay, but I have to tip him, don't I?" Jo rummaged through her pockets frantically for the crowns she'd exchanged at the airport. She stuffed some of her cash into his big, strong hands.

"No, too much." He looked down incredulously at the wad she'd handed over.

"Take it," she insisted, hoping the tip would put a smile on his stony—but still gorgeous—face.

He simply shrugged again and left, wheeling his dolly down the hall with nary a peep.

"What, no *thank you?*" Jo shrieked as she slammed the door after him.

"I don't think he understood you," Theresa offered.

"But I was speaking the *international* language!" Jo complained. "How could he *not*—"

"Can't talk! Clothes!" Caylin screeched.

Jo instantly brightened, and she and Caylin ripped open their boxes like kids on Christmas morning. Theresa lagged noticeably behind.

"Prada winter wear!" Jo squealed as she surveyed her duds, grateful that posing as a socialite guaranteed her a delicious designer wardrobe.

"I've got more of the Banana Republic thing going," Caylin said, pulling out tan wool pants and beige fisherman's sweaters. "I guess it's that whole Australian safari vibe."

"I'm the Gap girl, thank goodness," Theresa called, smiling brightly as she held up basic after basic.

Jo held up a cream-colored blouse and sighed. "Well, sisters, one thing's for sure."

"What's that?" Theresa asked.

"Even if we *don't* save the world, at least we'll look good."

feel like I'm in the middle of *Amadeus*," Caylin noted, Aussie accent in full effect as she led the way into the baroque city on a chilly Monday morning. "This city's a beaut, I tell ya!"

Peddlers made their way toward the town square, their pushcarts overflowing with everything from fruits and vegetables to handcrafted dolls and puppets. The spires and towers of the gorgeous Prague Castle dominated the skyline. Brightly painted houses—some dating back to the thirteenth century—lined the streets, contrasting with the stubborn gray sky.

Theresa smiled and nodded. "This place is about as far from Arizona as you can get, but it really *is* a beaut."

"It'd be a lot *more* of a beaut if it wasn't so freaking cold," Jo grumbled through chattering teeth. "You're sure you know where we're going?"

"Yep," Caylin affirmed. The instructions they retrieved from the safe last night informed them that Josefská, the narrow, cobbled street they were living on, led straight to the main square. There the St. Nikolai Theater and InterCorp were only a few meters away from each other. Despite Jo's grumblings, Caylin had a definite spring in her step.

"I can't believe we're finally *doing* something," she cheered.

"Yeah, freezing our butts off," Jo commented. "This little faux fur number is *not* cold-weather compatible."

"The Tower issued you a *long* coat, Jo," Theresa said. "It wouldn't kill you to wear it."

"But I can't cover up this gorgeous quilted mini!" Jo cried. "You might as well call the fashion police!"

In the square an ancient clock chimed ten.

The Spy Girls froze.

"That's our cue, Sheilas!" Caylin announced.

"Sheilas?" Jo asked.

"It's Aussie for 'girls,'" Caylin explained.

"I know," Jo said with a smile. "I saw *Crocodile Dundee* enough times. You don't have to lay it on so thick when it's just us."

"Yes, I do," Caylin argued. "This is like method acting. If I don't do it right here, how can I do it right when it counts?"

"Point taken," Theresa said. "Let's split up, sisters."

"Good luck, you guys," Jo said.

Theresa smiled nervously. "You too."

"G'day, mates!"

Each Spy Girl moved off in a different direction.

Each with a different mission.

Each wondering if she could pull it off.

"And this is the grand tour," Josef Capek droned as he walked Jo through the halls of InterCorp

Prague. "On the right, the employee break room."

"Exciting," Jo breathed. The first thing she had noticed about Josef Capek was his looks or, more specifically, his lack thereof. His short, stodgy frame, plain features, and receding hairline had thrilled Jo to pieces—not because she was into him but because she so *wasn't*. Since Capek's looks weren't the least bit lovable, Jo was able to concentrate solely on the InterCorp tour.

Of course, there was still that pesky matter of Ewan Gallagher to worry about. . . .

"You'll be required to perform general office duties—answering phones, running errands, that sort of thing," Capek continued as they walked down a long, narrow hall.

"That sounds fine to me," she said, effortlessly employing the accent she'd perfected while staying with relatives in Brazil.

As Capek directed her to her cubicle Jo was way tempted to ask where Mitchell von Strauss and Ewan Gallagher were. But Jo could tell that this was a busy office. Information would float through the air like confetti. She would quickly learn which bits were important and follow them through without arousing suspicion.

"This is your station," Capek announced as they approached a tiny cubicle already marked with a nameplate reading Selma Ribiero. "You will be assisting Alexander Gottwald, a vice president in charge of marketing. Why don't we meet him now?"

Jo nodded as she followed Capek down the hall.

She kept her eyes glued to door after door, hoping to see a plate with one of the nasty names. Nothing. She stifled a sigh of disappointment.

Then she saw it.

Mitchell von Strauss, right there in plain letters. And his office was within sight of her cube!

Jo's mind spun. It told her to bug his phone, make friends with his assistant, send him flowers, offer to play golf with him, do *anything* to get on the inside.

She flashed the stern-looking woman at the desk outside von Strauss's office a smile. Jo received a frown in return.

So much for *that* plan.

Alexander Gottwald's office was two down from von Strauss's. Jo regarded the imposing man behind the large, cherry-wood desk carefully. Gray-haired, distinguished, and Armani clad, he was the picture of sophistication as he extended a hand toward her.

"Welcome aboard," Gottwald said in accented English.

"I'm thrilled to be here, Mr. Gottwald," she said, blessing him with her best thousand-watt grin.

"Well, we'll definitely keep you busy," Gottwald said. "With the open-trade pact coming up, things are really reaching a boiling point."

No kidding, she thought, gazing blankly at him. "Open-trade pact?" she asked innocently.

"Yes—it's a very important event, but I'll let Josef fill you in on all the gory details," he explained. He gave her a stern look. "You should read the newspapers more, my dear."

"Yes, I know," she said, her voice full of shame.

"For now," Gottwald continued, "I'm expecting two important calls. One from Ewan Gallagher and one from Vienna. When they come through, make sure you find me immediately."

Jo's heart sped up at the mention of Ewan's name. She would actually be talking to him that day! Her first big break!

"I'll show her how to put calls through right away," Capek promised with an efficient nod.

"I look forward to working with you, Mr. Gottwald," Jo called as Capek ushered her out.

"Likewise, I'm sure, Selma," Gottwald replied, turning his attention back to his paperwork.

Moments after Capek trained her on the phone system and left her to her own devices, Jo's vibrating pager went off, jolting her from her thoughts.

She looked around casually. Seeing no one, she slipped the pager out of her pocket and glanced at it.

Go to ballet box office . . . Pick up ticket for tonight's performance . . . Uncle Sam.

"*Cool,*" she whispered.

"I'm Ottla Heydrich, director of ushers," a gray-haired woman told Caylin in fluent English. She extended a ring-adorned hand, and Caylin shook it briskly.

"Very nice to meet you," Caylin said. "Muriel Hewitt."

"Have a seat, Muriel." Ottla motioned to the chair in front of her desk.

39

While Ottla scanned "Muriel's" resume, Caylin looked around Ottla's office, which was tucked away in a far corner of the St. Nikolai Theater. It was a damp, dusky space filled with stacks of file folders, books, and ballet programs. Nothing too fascinating.

"Here from Australia, are you?" Ottla asked.

"You're not wrong about that!" Caylin laughed. "Aussie born and bred."

"Beautiful country," Ottla said offhandedly. She then took a deep breath. "As I'm sure you're aware, we're putting on *Swan Lake* right now. There are performances six nights a week. And our principal attraction, Anka Perdova, fills the seats night after night. Which means a St. Nikolai usher is a busy usher."

Caylin smiled, but she was bristling on the inside. She hated being talked down to. What was she, a third grader?

To Ottla she probably was.

"Let's go ahead and give you the tour," Ottla said. She rose from her chair and led Caylin out the door.

"It's a really beautiful theater," Caylin enthused. Hundreds of seats formed a sea of red velvet. Huge crystal chandeliers hung from above, and ornate moldings covered the high ceilings. The carpeting was bloodred, lined in gold. The stage was grandiose, and the air resonated with performances past. It simply oozed history.

"Yes, it is," Ottla agreed. "It was built in 1886, three years after the National Theater opened in 1883, and all renovations—up to the last one in

40

1988—have stayed true to the original design."

"Grouse!" Caylin exclaimed. Aussie for "very good."

Ottla gave her a confused look before handing her a piece of paper. "Here's a seating chart. You'll need to familiarize yourself with it immediately. You'll be seating people this evening."

"Righto," Caylin said, gazing down at the maze of numbers and boxes with confidence.

"We're getting ready to host all the dignitaries in town for the open-trade-pact signing in a week," Ottla said. "It will be the most important night of the year for us."

No kidding, Caylin thought grimly. "How exciting!" "Muriel" exclaimed.

"We'll definitely need your services that night," Ottla said, looking a bit worried. "The volume is going to be immense."

Caylin smiled. "Wouldn't miss it for the world!"

"The ballerinas are at a local school giving a concert this morning," Ottla explained, "so the theater is empty. Why don't you take advantage of it and acquaint yourself with the layout for a few hours?"

I'd like nothing better, Caylin thought.

Starting with backstage . . .

"So we have to touch up these three sets. The garden and great hall of Prince Siegfried's castle. And the lakeside. Do you have any questions, Tiffany?"

Hannah Shrum, a young American stagehand, was cheerfully training Theresa backstage. She'd already given Theresa a tour of the main theater.

41

Now they were getting down to the real nitty-gritty.

Theresa examined the mammoth sets warily. "Does it take long to do this?" she asked. The artistry was extremely detailed—like paint by numbers times a million. Since Theresa was way more proficient in keystrokes than brush strokes, she was a bit intimidated.

"Depends," Hannah said, eyeballing the gigantic, varied backdrops depicting huge oak trees and velvet couches and shimmering pools of water. "They have to be perfect every night, and sometimes the paint peels or cracks under the lights. The damage varies from show to show."

Theresa had already observed the out-of-date light system. But the lights weren't the only things that had captured her attention. She'd also noticed there weren't many people around. No ballerinas. Not even *Caylin* was anywhere to be seen. "How are the other people who work here?"

"Everyone is pretty cool as long as you stay out of their way," Hannah explained. "And not knowing how to speak Czech or Russian is a big handicap, although a lot gets communicated through pointing and hand signals. And even though our boss, Julius, can be a little temperamental at times, he's pretty laid-back once you get to know him. He's a British import—you know the type. Always wearing black leather pants and those clunky black boots. You'll meet him when he's back from that school thing."

Gotta snoop, Theresa thought. But how could she *not* be obvious? "Could you give me a backstage tour?" Theresa asked, cocking her head to the side. "I know you gave me that map earlier, but I'd like to see the real thing for myself. I don't want to get lost back there."

Hannah shrugged. "Why not?" she said, heading toward stage left and motioning for Theresa to follow.

"Here's the costume department . . . props . . . lighting . . ."

Hannah reeled off a laundry list of offices as they strolled down the dim hall and slowly passed each one. Their heavy footsteps broke the eerie silence. Theresa wrinkled her nose at the dank, musty smell that hung in the air—the walls were as dingy and water-stained as the ones in her new apartment building. The doors were constructed of heavy gray steel, giving the space an industrial feel. Theresa carefully tried to commit each door to memory.

"Here's Anka Perdova's dressing room," Hannah said.

A surge of adrenaline flowed through Theresa. She just knew she had to get in there . . . *somehow*.

I hope I can keep all these numbers straight, Caylin prayed as the audience started to file in for the evening's performance. Although she'd memorized most of the sections with no problem, she was still a bit freaked she'd mess something up. After all, an accent, alias, *and* new job were a lot for a girl to juggle all at once.

But after about twenty seatings Caylin's anxiety subsided. In fact, she found she was even enjoying herself. Seeing all the people dressed in tuxedos and long, flowing, elegant dresses was somewhat magical. Walking up and down the stairs again and again and again was way better than a workout on the StairMaster. Her assignment *did* have its fringe benefits, she had to admit.

"Seat forty-two-D," a familiar voice said, yanking Caylin from her thoughts.

"Jo!" Caylin gasped. "What are you doing here?"

"My *uncle* gave me a ticket," Jo said with a wink.

"Right this way," Caylin said, trying to keep her expression even in case anyone was watching.

"I never saw Ewan or von Strauss even once today," Jo hissed as she followed Caylin down the stairs.

"My day's been a snooze, too," Caylin whispered. "All aisle letters and seat numbers."

"Ewan was supposed to call my boss, but he never did," Jo said. "Talk about false hope."

Caylin pointed toward Jo's assigned seat. "Let's hope Theresa's having better luck than we are."

"We need one last touch-up on that tree over there, Tiffany," Julius demanded moments before curtain. "Go in the supply closet and get some more paint, quick!"

"No problem," Theresa said, frantically sprinting to fetch the paint.

What a jerk! As far as Theresa could tell, Julius was nothing more than a short, ugly man with an even shorter and uglier personality. But maybe he'd grow on her . . . like a fungus! If he weren't head of the props and lighting departments, Julius would be one loathsome and useless human being.

She rounded the corner near the supply closet and slammed into something so forcefully, she landed on her butt.

"Whoa!" she muttered, shaking the Tweety birds away. "I'm really sorry."

Theresa stood up shakily and saw dark, almond-shaped eyes and beautiful black hair pulled back in a supertight bun. A tight white tutu on a body that was one of the most muscular and graceful she had ever seen.

Anka Perdova!

"Oh n-no, it's y-you," Theresa stammered. "I didn't even see—"

"Stupid American," Anka spat. She shoved Theresa aside and headed straight to her dressing room.

The door slammed.

Theresa stood there, gaping. For someone who danced so beautifully, Anka sure was nasty! The ballerina had looked so nice on video, signing autographs and smiling.

Maybe she should think about changing her name to *Sybil* Perdova, Theresa thought. Either that or double up on the Midol!

As the lights dimmed, Jo settled back in her seat and took a deep breath.

Her father had always loved the ballet. It was a soft side few people saw of the no-nonsense, hard-line judge. He had always claimed that it re-laxed him. Transported him.

So as the first note of music sounded Jo closed her eyes and let herself go. When she opened her lids, every concrete thought in her head was whisked away by the delicate beauty and grace of the dancers' movements. The ballerinas were talented, but Anka Perdova truly stole the show.

She glided across the stage effortlessly, leaping to the heavens and practically flying through the air. Uncle Sam wasn't kidding when he said she was the troupe's principal attraction. As far as Jo was concerned, Anka earned that title in spades the first five seconds of her performance.

It was hard to believe that in a week's time, this entire theater could be a bloodbath. How could InterCorp do such a thing?

The mere thought of InterCorp made Jo sick. Money. Power. All these things were bought with blood. Jo learned that at a very young age.

The ballet played on. Peaceful. Beautiful.

Seeing the talented ballerinas in action made Jo all the more determined to stop InterCorp and save Prime Minister Karkovic. She was willing to do whatever it took. For the sake of world peace and for the memory of her father.

When the lights went up for intermission, Jo looked back and snuck a smile at Caylin, who was in the rear of the auditorium, directing people to the lobby. After Caylin met her gaze, Jo scanned the room for a glimpse of Theresa. She didn't see her.

Live and Let Spy

But she did notice a gaggle of small children gathered near the stage, lined up for Anka's autograph.

How cute, Jo thought. But while watching Anka, tight-lipped and businesslike, scrawl her name on the kids' programs, Jo's eyes narrowed. Something didn't feel quite right.

She grabbed her satin clutch and hurriedly fished out her mascara cam—a minicamera concealed in a trademark pink-and-green tube of Great Lash, courtesy of The Tower.

Jo snapped a few shots just to be on the safe side.

She couldn't quite put her finger on it yet, but something was definitely wrong with this picture.

I wish we could have stopped at the Malostranská kavárna," Theresa declared as she plopped down on the couch in their flat on Monday evening. "That's where Kafka used to hang out in the twenties."

"You know we can't be seen in public together," Jo reminded her, biting into a grilled cheese sandwich.

"I know," Theresa replied. "It just would've been nice."

The Spy Girls had made their way separately back to their flat after the ballet. Theresa had suggested that they use this time every night to share their information and theories. Though on this first night, they didn't have much.

"Leave it to you to know about who ate somewhere a zillion years ago," Caylin muttered through her ab crunches. Her blond hair was tied back in a ponytail, and sweat beaded her brow.

"So I like Kafka," Theresa replied. "So what?"

"The only person's eating habits I care about at the moment are *mine*," Jo said, chomping the grilled cheese. "I'm starvin', Marvin, and I can't deal with the cuisine. Can you believe they actually sell *deer* in the supermarkets here?"

"Well, at least you're not starving *and* in pain," Caylin said, glaring angrily at her Italian leather pumps, which lay on the floor a few feet away. "Those heels nearly killed me tonight."

"You'll live," Jo replied. "So what do you all think is up with this Anka chick?"

"What do you mean what's up with her?" Caylin asked in confusion, finishing her crunches and sitting up.

"Something's not right," Jo said. "I can't explain it, but when she was signing autographs, something weird was going on. Like she was all tight-lipped and sour faced. Nothing like she was in the video we saw."

"I accidentally bumped into her before the performance and she nearly took my head off," Theresa divulged. "She gave me a dirty look, then called me a stupid American."

"That doesn't fit what we know about her personality," Caylin said.

"That's what I'm saying," Jo insisted. "Something just doesn't fit here. I took a few snaps of her with the mascara cam. Maybe they'll tell us something."

"Psychic factor of ten!" Theresa exclaimed. "After my run-in with *Cranka*, I shot a video of her performance."

"No way," Jo replied, smiling.

"Way," Theresa said. "I just clipped my porta-cam

to a broom propped against stage left and voilà, it was lights, camera, action."

She fished the black porta-cam from her coat pocket and showed it off—only a quarter of a pound and the size of a pack of gum. She placed it on the coffee table in front of them and sat down.

"Let's run it all through the video software," Jo suggested, slipping her mascara cam out of her red satin clutch.

Theresa agreed and set up her new laptop in front of them. She uncoiled the digital camera adapter and plugged the mascara cam into a video port in the back of the computer.

"This stuff is so cool," Theresa remarked, her eyes fixed and intent on the hardware. "Digital cameras are going to make conventional film completely obsolete, I'm telling you."

"Guess I better sell that photo stock," Caylin muttered.

Theresa punched at the keyboard furiously. Finally a crisp image of the theater appeared on the screen.

"Good shot," Caylin remarked.

"Good seat," Jo replied. "Wish I had that seat for the season."

Theresa clicked through the shots—four in all—of Anka Perdova signing autographs. There she was, grim and snarly.

"See what I mean?" Jo pointed out. "Not a happy camper."

"I see that she's grumpy," Caylin said. "But that's about it."

"Let's zoom in on Anka," Theresa suggested, her brow furrowed in concentration. She moved the mouse and clicked away. Anka suddenly doubled in size.

"Nice pen," Caylin pointed out. "Mont Blanc."

"I'm so impressed," Theresa replied dryly.

"Wait!" Jo cried.

"What is it?"

"Can you call up that very first video we saw of Anka?" Jo asked. "The one where she's signing autographs with the kids?"

"Yeah," Theresa replied.

"Can you put the images side by side?"

"Yeah. What's the deal, Jo?"

"Just do it!" Jo ordered. "Hurry!"

Theresa clicked away. In minutes a still picture of the smiling Anka was next to the scowling one.

"Not much difference," Caylin stated. "Except she has a nice smile."

Jo chuckled. Then outright giggled.

"Jo?" Theresa asked.

"What is it?" Caylin demanded.

"Don't you *see* it?" Jo wondered.

"See what?"

"Right there in front of you!" Jo said, pointing and laughing. "That's the answer right there!"

"*What* is?" Caylin growled.

Theresa's jaw dropped open. "I see it!"

52

"See *what?*" Caylin continued, her face reddening. "You two are killing me!"

"Cay," Jo explained, "you noticed the pen before. Compare the two pens."

Caylin took a moment. "They're the exact same pen, Jo. Exact. Except . . ."

"Yeah?" Jo asked hopefully, sharing a smile with Theresa.

"Oh, wow!" Caylin exclaimed, a lightbulb practically flashing on above her head. "That's it!"

"You see it, too?" Theresa asked.

"Her *hands!*" Caylin said. "In the happy picture she's left-handed. In the nasty picture *she's right-handed!*"

"You win Final Jeopardy," Jo remarked.

"Well, maybe she's—" Caylin's brow wrinkled in thought.

"Ambidextrous?" Theresa finished.

"Yeah!"

"No. Anka Perdova's dossier says that she has been left-handed since childhood," Theresa said.

The Spy Girls shared a knowing look.

"That proves it, then," Theresa said.

"Right," Jo replied. "This can only mean one thing."

Caylin nodded. "The Anka we saw tonight is an imposter!"

"Good work, ladies," Uncle Sam complimented, his shadowy silhouette shimmering in the aquarium's screen. "I'll pass this info on."

53

"If InterCorp installed an Anka look-alike," Theresa said, "think how easy it would be to assassinate Prime Minister Karkovic. She'd have a clear shot from the stage. Bang, bang—he's a goner, and the real Anka—wherever she may be—is left holding the bag."

"Maybe InterCorp kidnapped her," Jo suggested.

"It's a theory," Uncle Sam replied.

"Maybe, maybe not," Caylin countered as she juggled a squirt bottle of water between her hands. "I have dancing experience, and if that woman's a killer, she's a darn good dancer, too."

"It *is* hard to believe InterCorp could find someone that good," Theresa agreed. "And who looks so much like Anka."

"Hard to believe, yes, but not impossible," Jo reasoned. "Especially with the dough InterCorp's got. And hello—plastic surgery?"

"Plastic surgery is *that* advanced?" Caylin asked. "I mean, this is *Face/Off* territory."

"Uncle Sam?" Theresa probed. "Is it possible? I mean, has The Tower done this sort of thing?"

Uncle Sam remained silent.

Jo shuddered. "Eew, creepy."

"Wait a sec. What if the real Anka has been murdered?" Theresa wondered. "That changes everything."

Jo shook her head. "She probably has to be alive if they're going to pin the assassination on her."

54

"Either that or the look-alike is the fall gal," Caylin offered.

"I agree with Jo on this one," Uncle Sam stated. "Odds are that Anka Perdova is alive and somewhere in Prague."

"Why do you think that?" Jo asked.

"If she's going to take the fall, she needs to be close to the scene—that way she can be switched with the imposter without delay," Uncle Sam explained. "Finding the real Anka Perdova is now a priority."

Caylin grinned. Her whole body felt wired with anticipation. "Now we're cooking with fire!"

"Find out what you can, ladies," Uncle Sam said. "In the meantime, Theresa, I have something specific in mind for you."

"Shoot," she said, her calm voice not betraying her excitement. She rested her electronic notebook in her lap, hands hovering.

"Anka Perdova has an on-line account with Artech, a European carrier," Uncle Sam explained. "Our records show that she has been on-line regularly from the theater. As recently as yesterday, as a matter of fact."

"Hmmm. The imposter knows her way around the web, huh?" Theresa noted.

"Does she have a computer in her dressing room?" Jo asked.

"Laptop, probably," Theresa replied, typing the info into her notebook. "She could be communicating with her boss."

55

"Exactly," Uncle Sam agreed. "Theresa, I want you to get into her dressing room and make a copy of whatever's on her hard drive. Files, incoming mail, the works. She might slip up and give us something good."

Theresa chuckled nervously. "Uh, not to be negative or anything . . . I mean, the hack is a snap. But how exactly am I supposed to break into her dressing room?"

"I was hoping you would ask that," Uncle Sam replied confidently. "Under the lamp in your bedroom you'll find a little item that just might help you out. Go get it, please."

Theresa hurried into her bedroom and returned with a key ring. It held one key and a square plastic attachment that resembled a car alarm remote. "Here it is."

"That key unlocks eighty percent of locks in the world," Uncle Sam explained. "It should work on Anka's door."

"Cool," Jo responded, snagging it from Theresa's grasp. "Can we keep it?"

"Absolutely not," Uncle Sam replied. "And I'd be careful how you handle that key ring, Jo."

"Why?" Jo asked. "Will it blow up?"

"No. But if you snap your fingers, the metal edge of that plastic remote becomes the business end of a very potent stun gun. The voltage is enough to stop a two-hundred-fifty-pound man."

Theresa yanked the key ring back. She stared at the dull metal plate on the stun gun and chuckled nervously. "Knowing my luck, I'll run into a guy who weighs two fifty-one."

Jo was sitting at the ballet during intermission, wearing a flowing green velvet dress. As she scanned the stage for the fake Anka she spotted Ewan Gallagher lurking by the front row.

This was her chance to meet him!

Practically floating on air, she made her way down toward the stage. As she got closer his immaculately combed blond hair came into focus. As did his square jaw and handsome, chiseled face.

He turned to speak to her, his ice blue eyes locking on hers.

Jo's heart pounded in her chest. She felt her cheeks flush. She awkwardly introduced herself as Selma Ribiero.

Ewan smiled and extended his hand. "Hello, Jo Carreras."

Her jaw dropped open in surprise.

How did he know her real name?

"Uh . . . my name is Selma. Selma Ribiero."

"Whatever you say, Jo," Ewan replied, his grin menacing. "Why don't we go meet the prime minister?"

Ewan grabbed her elbow and led her forcefully along the row of seats.

"Karkovic?" she asked, confused and panicked. "What's going on? Let me go!"

As they approached the prime minister the people around him—including his bodyguards—parted so they could get through. Jo recognized Karkovic immediately. She'd seen his picture a thousand times.

The prime minister rose to greet them, extending his hand and smiling. "Hello, Jo," he said, covering her hand with his. Karkovic's grip was firm and strong.

"Wha-what?" she stammered.

How did he know her real name, too?

He laughed and released her hand. But when he did, Jo heard a loud, earsplitting boom.

Something zipped by her ear. Too fast to see. A supersonic wasp. There was a simultaneous thunk. Like slapping meat with your bare hand.

Jo screamed, bewildered, as Karkovic was flung backward in agonizingly slow motion.

Blood erupted from his tuxedo shirt. Dazzling red on white.

He'd been shot in the heart.

When he landed in his theater seat, Jo saw a clear image of the wounded man.

It was not Karkovic.

It was *her father* lying there, blood pumping steadily out of his limp, lifeless form.

Jo sat up ramrod straight.

She blinked, her breath ragged. The room was dark. Shadowy.

She was in her bedroom in the flat. In Prague.

Safe.

It was just a dream—a bad dream.

While she struggled to catch her breath, Jo had

58

a sudden image of her father in his casket, so ashen and alien to her fourteen-year-old eyes.

She let out a deep breath and forced herself to lie back down. She gripped her pillow with her fists and made a silent vow.

She wasn't going to let Prime Minister Karkovic's family go through what she had gone through.

No way.

Who could that be?" Caylin wondered as the phone in her room bleeped loudly on Tuesday morning. She wiped the sleep from her eyes and picked up the phone, careful to use her Aussie accent. "G'day."

"Hello, is Muriel there?"

"This is she," Caylin replied.

"It's Ottla calling," her boss said. "I'm afraid I didn't mention it yesterday with all the first-day confusion, but you don't need to be in until one o'clock from now on. I just wanted you to report early yesterday to get the seat numbers down, but it seems you got through your first night with flying colors."

"If there's anything that needs to be done around the office, I can always blow in early," Caylin offered, positively itching to nose around for some info on Anka.

"Well, I had planned to have you do some light office work in the afternoons and usher in the evenings from here on out, so there's really no need for you to come in early," Ottla said. "Unless, of course, you just want to."

"Righto," Caylin chirped. "Ten it is."

"Uh . . . okay," Ottla said.

But Caylin didn't particularly care if she confused Ottla or not. She was on a mission to find Anka's whereabouts, and digging up any information would definitely be a good start.

Time was already running out.

"He's working us like dogs!" Theresa whispered to Hannah. Julius had been watching them with barely concealed anger all morning as they touched up each and every set. Unfortunately none of their efforts had been good enough to win his approval thus far.

Theresa dropped her brush on the tree she was retouching and wiped her forehead with the back of her hand, utterly exhausted. "Man, what I wouldn't give to be in Jo's and Caylin's shoes right now," she muttered to herself. "This is slave labor."

As she finished perfecting the tree's paint job Theresa caught a glimpse of Fake Anka leaving her dressing room. Theresa checked her paint-splattered watch: 12:05.

"Finally," she whispered.

Lunchtime for the prima donna. That meant Fake Anka would be gone for at least an hour. Theresa shot Julius her hungriest look. Give us a lunch break, give us a lunch break, she silently commanded, hoping he'd catch her Psychic Friends Network vibes and let her get down to Spy Girl business.

Live and Let Spy

"*Ach,* go and eat, you people," Julius finally growled. "Perhaps food will make you better painters!"

Theresa let out a huge sigh and dropped her brush into the thinner.

"Wanna join me, Tiffany?" Hannah asked, grabbing her coat from the corner. "There's a café down the street that has unbelievable soup."

"Thanks, but I need to run some errands," Theresa said with an apologetic shrug. If breaking into someone's office counted as an errand, then she wasn't *totally* lying, she reasoned.

The second Julius made his exit, it was show time. Looking around the halls to make sure the coast was clear, Theresa slipped into the costume closet, her heart pounding.

She locked the door and frantically searched the crowded racks for the right size bodysuit, tights, and slippers.

Deep breath, Theresa, deep breath! she commanded herself as she slid out of her Gap wear and into her makeshift ballerina suit.

As she pulled her hair haphazardly back into a severe bun Theresa reminded herself to grab the key ring and computer disks from her jeans.

It would totally suck if she forgot those.

She extracted them from her pocket, hoping she hadn't forgotten anything else.

Theresa took a deep breath. "Now or never."

She slowly turned the doorknob and poked her head out. Looked right. Then left.

The hall was empty.

She quickly slipped out of the costume closet and tiptoed down the hall.

I sure don't feel like a ballerina, she thought.

Anka's dressing room door was in sight. Just slip in and get the job done. Nice and neat. Better than Bond.

She pulled the magic key ring out and fingered the key. Her sweaty palms made the metal slick.

"Calm down," she told herself.

She began the final steps toward the door.

A maintenance man rounded the corner right in front of her. A surge of panic swept through her.

He gazed straight ahead and whistled softly. His belly jostled with each thick step.

Oh no!

Theresa ducked her head immediately. She held her chin in a southbound position and continued strolling down the hall.

Just another ballerina . . .

She prayed the maintenance guy wouldn't see her face and bust her undercover mission wide open. She knew he'd seen her around. She knew he knew who Tiffany was.

His hulking shape tromped by.

Theresa caught a whiff of tobacco. And intense BO.

Ugh! It was so bad, she had to cover her nose.

But thankfully the man's footsteps grew fainter and fainter.

Theresa sighed, grateful for the breath of fresh air. She was safe—for the moment. She chanced a glance over her shoulder. The maintenance man was gone. The hall was clear again.

"Man, did he reek!" she muttered as she back-tracked to Anka's dressing room. Lifting the key up to her pursed lips and kissing it for good luck, she silently prayed Anka's lock wasn't one of the twenty percent in the world the key wouldn't open.

Slowly sliding the cold metal into the ancient knob, she held her breath and turned the key ever so slightly.

Nothing. It didn't budge.

New panic pumped through her. What if she couldn't get in?

She tried again. It still wouldn't budge.

Suddenly the sound of approaching footsteps filled the silence.

Theresa's mouth went dry as cotton. She froze.

What was she going to do now?

"Here's a list of people who will be at Sunday's open-trade-pact signing, Ms. Ribiero," Alexander Gottwald told Jo as he handed her a thick stack of paper right before lunch. "The caterer needs a final head count, so confirm these RSVPs ASAP."

"A-OK," she replied.

Gottwald didn't seem to get it.

As he disappeared into his office Jo quickly scanned the list. The name "Karkovic, Gogol" jumped out immediately.

He'll be dead meat if we don't stop this, Jo thought. Less than six days were left until the—

Someone cleared his throat behind her. Jo turned. Ewan Gallagher!

He was even more gorgeous than in her nightmares!

Jo forced herself to stay cool, showing no signs of recognition—or lust—as she scoped him out.

Ewan's gelled blond hair was in tousled waves atop his head. His cold blue eyes were like icicles boring into her own. When he smiled, two adorable dimples dotted his cheeks.

And the devastating final touch—his Armani was a *perfect* fit.

"Can I help you?" Jo asked coolly.

"I'm Ewan Gallagher, director of international relations," he said. "And you are?"

She stuck out a Versace-covered arm and shook his hand. "Selma Ribiero, intern," she said, flashing him her pearly whites in what she hoped was a *friendly* and not *flirtatious* way. "Anything I can do for you?"

He smiled. "Actually, I was wondering if you could type up some memos for me. My secretary has gone home sick. Twenty-four-hour bug, we hope."

"No problem," Jo said, locked in his magnetic gaze.

"Can you type the top two in French?" he asked, eyebrow cocked.

Jo lowered her eyelids halfway. "I think I can handle that."

"I am impressed, Miss Ribiero," he replied, slipping a hand casually into his pocket. "Most Americans can speak only English."

"Well, I got around quite a bit in my youth," Jo explained, flashing her best smile again. "It's a small world."

"Indeed," Ewan replied. "And yet we receive small surprises every day."

"I surprise you?"

Ewan chuckled. "Perhaps you should get back to your memos, Miss Ribiero."

"Call me J—just Selma."

Oops. Steady, girl.

"Selma," Ewan repeated, eyes twinkling. "A very pretty name."

"Thank you," Jo replied, even though she *hated* the name.

He checked his watch. "Now I must go. Feel free to drop the memos in my in box when you get the chance."

"Will *you* be in?"

Ewan smirked. "I doubt it, Selma. I get around quite a bit myself."

He turned and strode down the hallway. He turned the corner and was gone.

Jo let out a sigh. Then smiled slyly.

"I think I got him," she whispered.

Just open! Theresa silently pleaded as she tried Anka's dressing room lock.

Still nothing. Nothing but approaching footsteps and the pounding of her own heart.

The footsteps grew nearer and nearer. Faster, faster . . .

One more time, she told herself. Shutting her eyes, she tried to envision the door opening easily as she turned the key in the lock. Not that it would work, but . . .

It did. The tarnished knob turned and she was in.

Theresa quickly and quietly shut the door behind her. She pressed her ear against it, listening.

Her heartbeat intensified as the steps grew louder.

"I'm so busted," she whispered.

But the footsteps faded.

Whew! This spy business would kill her yet.

"Okay, Anka—or whoever you are, where do you keep your laptop?" Theresa wondered out loud.

She scanned the desktop, the floor, the bookshelves. No computer anywhere to be found.

"Don't tell me she took it with her," she muttered, flinging open every drawer in sight. She could have sworn Fake Anka didn't have any bags with her when she left.

"Okay, baby, be here." She yanked open the bottom desk drawer. There, underneath a tattered Euro edition of *Vogue,* was the elusive PC.

"Gotcha."

She plugged in the modem and hit the on/off button. As the familiar "ding" sounded and the smiling disk appeared on-screen, Theresa smiled, too—from the pure rush of adrenaline she felt. She felt like that chick from *Hackers*—brainy, brazen, *and* babelicious.

"Internet provider, where are you . . . there you are," she said, double clicking on its accompanying icon. Her motions were fast-forward and precise now. She was in the zone.

"Okay, decoder disk, make me proud." She placed her floppy into the computer's disk drive. A wordy prompt popped up on-screen. Theresa clicked "find password" and the decoder disk went to work. Hundreds of password combinations filled the screen in seconds.

"What's it going to be?" Theresa wondered. "Egomaniac? Prima donna? Imposterina?"

But no. The magic word was *pirouette.*

"Gotcha, part *deux!*" She replaced the decoder disk with a blank to copy the hard drive. The computer went to work, and Theresa leaned back to take a deep breath.

Just as the doorknob rattled.

She whirled around and gasped at the sound.

70

Indeed, the knob was rattling back and forth. Theresa's blood ran cold.

Someone was coming in.

And she, smart girl that she was, *forgot to lock the door behind her.*

"Oh, *pretzels.*"

Theresa knew she had only one option. Her clammy hands frantically groped for the stun-gun key chain. And her eyes closed as she anticipated the absolute worst.

Depression set in as Jo went over the memos Ewan had asked her to type. She thought perhaps she might pick up some vital information from them. But no such luck. Reading the memos had been exciting for the first five seconds, but the thrill had long since vanished.

"Dear Sir, I must decline your dinner invitation," she read aloud as she typed away, rolling her eyes at the sheer inanity of it all. But after she printed the first letter, she decided to make a copy of it on her hard drive.

"You never know. . . ."

On the way to Ewan's office Jo spotted Mitchell von Strauss approaching. He looked exactly the same as he had in the video—tall, silver haired, and distinguished. She noted his serious expression as he slipped into his office and quickly shut the door.

"In the flesh at last," she whispered, slightly bummed about not scoring a personal intro. All in due time, she told herself. All in due time.

Jo was surprised to find Ewan at his desk. She smiled and entered without knocking.

"I thought you were out globe-trotting," she purred, dropping the completed memos on his desk.

He smiled at the sight of her. "Unfortunately work must intrude." His eyes scanned her up and down as he put the memos aside. "You're a lifesaver, Selma."

Jo blushed despite herself. "Don't mention it," she said, trying to keep her tone in that happy medium between professional and playful. "If you need anything else, you know where to find me."

"That I do," Ewan said, grinning wider.

She nodded and turned on her stilettos to exit without another word. But as Jo strolled out the door she felt Ewan's gaze upon her, watching her every step.

Theresa secured a vise grip on her stun gun.

The dressing room door slooowly inched open, creaking eerily the entire way.

Theresa fought off the urge to yell or scream or crawl under the desk and hide. She had to stand tall. Stay calm.

Yeah, right, she thought. Easier said than done.

A male head became visible through the partially opened doorway. Not Anka, thank goodness. But who was it?

The smell hit her nose.

Intense BO.

The maintenance man!

Theresa immediately turned her head so that he

would only be able to see her from behind. The tutu. The tight bun of hair.

"*Prosím,*" he mumbled—obviously in Czech.

She said nothing and shooed him away with her hand, hoping he'd just exit without an argument.

"*Prosím!*" he repeated. Only this time he punctuated the foreign statement with "Anka."

He thought she was Anka!

"Go away!" she ordered in her nastiest voice.

Ding!

Theresa jumped as the computer sounded. She could still feel the maintenance man hovering in the doorway. Trying not to shake, Theresa hit eject and slowly removed the disk from the drive.

The maintenance man uttered something in an angry tone and slammed the door.

"Man, do you *stink!*" she declared. Relief flooded her as she snapped Anka's laptop shut and placed it back precisely where she'd found it.

Seconds later she stuck her head out the door, looked right then left, and dashed to the costume closet, changing into her clothes as rapidly as the models she'd seen backstage at her mother's runway shows.

She exited the closet, bun halfway undone and attire slightly disheveled.

Someone clunked around the corner.

"Julius!" she called, trying to sound nonchalant.

"What were you doing in there?" he asked suspiciously.

"Uh, just looking for a safe place to stash my

purse," Theresa replied innocently. "I, uh, went to the bank over lunch."

"Well," he snarled, "that room is off-limits."

Theresa triumphantly ran her fingers over the disk in her front pocket, giving Julius her most innocent "Who, me?" smile. "Sorry, Julius. It won't happen again. I *promise.*"

"When Ottla told me the files were a wreck, she wasn't kidding," Caylin grumbled as she waded through a muddled sea of paperwork. Although she had gone through nearly every file in the office, Caylin hadn't yet run across one on Anka Perdova. And since she'd located a file for every single other ballerina, the absence of Anka's was a major red flag.

When Ottla returned from lunch, Caylin approached her.

"I've noticed some of these file folders are ragged and mismarked," Caylin stated, "and I'd like to dice them and create new ones for the troupe. Is there any way I could get a list of the performers, just so I don't leave anyone out?"

Ottla blessed her with a smile of approval. "Aren't we the industrious one?" She immediately sat down at her desk and printed out a list.

"And you know," Caylin continued innocently, "I can't seem to find a folder for Anka Perdova at all."

Ottla shrugged. "It must have been misplaced, I guess."

Try stolen, Caylin thought with a frustrated frown.

* * *

74

Live and Let Spy

"You guys have been *busy*," Danielle said as she, Uncle Sam, and the Spy Girls shared a conference call on the aquarium phone later that evening.

"No kidding," Theresa replied. "Three heart attacks in one day is enough for me, thank you very much."

"Did you find anything that looked suspicious on the hard drive, Theresa?" Uncle Sam inquired.

"Sure did," Theresa said with a triumphant smile. "The only thing out of the ordinary was a piece of e-mail received yesterday morning. The subject was 'Danny Thugs I.'"

"What did it say?" Danielle asked, her image expanding as she moved closer to the video cam in anticipation.

"It said, 'Once hit, lights out,'" Theresa recited, looking down at her crumpled piece of paper. "'Escape route A. Subject in the dark. No implication.'"

"What's your take on that?" Uncle Sam asked.

"Obviously," Theresa replied, "'once hit, lights out' means once Karkovic is hit, the theater will go black."

"Good theory," Uncle Sam said. "Go on."

"'Escape route A' is a preplanned route for Fake Anka after she shoots Karkovic. 'Subject in the dark' I take to mean that the real Anka is clueless over who her kidnapper is. And 'No implication' means no consequences will be suffered because the kidnapper will replace Fake Anka with the real Anka immediately." Theresa took a breath, then stared directly into the fish lens. "So, what do you think?"

"I think it sounds like you're right on all counts," Uncle Sam said. "Very good job, Theresa."

"But what does 'Danny Thugs I' mean?" Jo asked.

Caylin shrugged. "Do you think someone named Danny could have Anka?"

"Or 'thugs' could mean there's more than one," Jo added.

"And I was thinking—since all this is going down at the theater, do you suppose the real Anka is being kept in there?" Theresa suggested. "It seems like the most convenient place, especially if the kidnapper—or kidnappers—plan to switch the two Ankas as soon as possible."

"It's possible," Uncle Sam said, "but we'll just need to keep our eyes and ears open and investigate to see if our theories are valid or not." He paused. "Anyone else make any progress?"

"Well," Caylin began, "I found out there's no file on Anka Perdova." She launched into the story of how every troupe member had one except Anka and that Ottla didn't seem too concerned about it. "I think someone stole it."

"Good to know," Uncle Sam said. "Keep up your probe. How about your day, Jo?"

"Well, I got the RSVP list for the treaty signing," she announced, holding up the copy she'd made for herself in front of the camera.

"Hey, I know," Caylin exclaimed, "why don't you check to see if there are any Dans or Dannys on the list? That could be our 'Danny Thugs I.'"

"Good idea," Uncle Sam replied.

Jo scanned the list. "There's one Dan—Dan Fields," she said, "and one Daniela—Daniela

76

Fuentes. No one with the last name 'Daniel' or 'Daniels.' I'll find out who they are in the morning and see if they're legit."

"Sounds good," Uncle Sam affirmed. "Anything else?"

Jo read Ewan's memos aloud.

"They don't sound like much," Uncle Sam surmised when she was done, "but it's good you've established contact with one of the key players."

"I'll bet she has," Caylin teased.

Theresa rolled her eyes. "Don't tell me you've got a crush on this guy *already!*"

Jo scowled. "Mind your own espionage, girls. I've got things under control."

"You mean under your spell," Caylin corrected.

"What can I say?" Jo replied. "I don't spy and tell."

"That's quite enough, ladies," Uncle Sam scolded. "Jo, I don't have to remind you of your mission parameters, do I?"

"Absolutely not," Jo replied, shooting a scowl at Theresa and Caylin.

"Speaking of Gallagher," Danielle interjected, "how about bugging his and von Strauss's phones?"

"Jo, see what you can do about that," Uncle Sam ordered. "The bugs are in the kitchen in the canister marked 'flour.' And Caylin, I'd like you to gain access to the theater's executive offices. They're not in use right now in preparation for some renovation project, but they still hold files there. Once you get in, ransack the area for anything pertaining to Anka Perdova."

"I'm on it," Caylin said.

"And I'll keep checking Anka's e-mail and try to locate a floor plan or any secret hideaways backstage," Theresa promised. "Who knows—maybe the true Anka is right under our noses."

"That would be nice," Caylin said solemnly.

"Remember your assignments, Spy Girls," Uncle Sam commanded. "Or Prime Minister Karkovic will end up like Abraham Lincoln."

"Yeah," Theresa replied. "Shot in an old theater for reasons that make no sense at all."

Yes, this is Selma Ribiero from InterCorp Prague," Jo said into the phone as she sat in her cubicle on Wednesday morning. "Will Daniela Fuentes be attending the open-trade-pact signing?"

Jo posed the question in Portuguese, as she had noticed the international code preceding Ms. Fuentes's phone number was 55—Brazil. After Ms. Fuentes's assistant answered in the affirmative, Jo asked, "And could you please give me her full professional title?"

"Vice president of international affairs, Brazilian Council," the assistant replied, her tone implying it was a very stupid question.

Jo politely thanked her and hung up. Then, after making sure no one was within earshot, Jo immediately placed a call to the Brazilian Council to find out if Ms. Fuentes was indeed legit.

"Yes, this is Selma Ribiero from *Noticias Sudamericanas*," Jo lied to the Brazilian Council receptionist in Portuguese. "I'm fact checking an article about the open-trade-pact signing and was wondering if you could verify the spelling of Daniela Fuentes's name and the exact wording of her official title?"

It was exactly the same. Jo crossed Daniela Fuentes off her list.

Next Dan Fields of the good ol' USA. When a woman answered with "Dan Fields's office," Jo went into her usual spiel.

"Yes, he will be attending," the secretary confirmed.

"And can I get his official title?" she asked.

"Head foreign correspondent," she replied, *New York Chronicle.*"

"Thank you," Jo said, punching the *New York Chronicle* into her computer to see if Dan Fields's name was on their official web site. After a few keystrokes "Dan Fields, head foreign correspondent" popped up on the virtual masthead.

"Oh, well," Jo muttered with a frustrated sigh. But one look at the clock was enough to perk her up.

12:30 P.M. Ewan and Mitchell von Strauss would be at lunch.

"Get out your Raid, boys and girls," she whispered, dropping two pea-size surveillance devices in her pocket. "'Cause you got bugs."

Jo grabbed a thick stack of files and marched down the hall, looking busy.

Mitchell's office door was wide open and his secretary nowhere in sight. With a deep breath Jo pulled a bug out of her pocket.

"Here goes nothing," she whispered, heading for Mitchell's office. When a cleaning lady passed her way in the hall, Jo gave her a brisk nod and continued confidently on.

As she entered Mitchell's domain she smoothed

her Dior suit and left the door just slightly ajar—a closed office door usually sent up a red flag of suspicion in the business world, she had learned.

Jo picked up Mitchell's receiver and expertly installed the bugging device, her movements both fluid and precise. Bugging Mitchell's phone gave Jo the same rush she got behind the wheel of a race car—her blood pumped, her mind raced.

But when she heard Mitchell's secretary's voice seconds after she placed the receiver in its cradle, Jo felt more like she had hit a gigantic speed bump.

"May I help you?" the secretary inquired, her tone nasal and accusatory.

"Just dropping off these papers for Mr. von Strauss," Jo said, exactly as she'd rehearsed.

"With the door practically closed?" the secretary asked warily.

"Oh, did the door close behind me?" Jo recited from memory. "Must have been a draft."

"I'll make sure he gets the papers, then," the secretary promised, ceremoniously motioning her out.

"Thanks a mil," Jo purred, smiling in victory. But before she allowed herself to feel too cocky, she had one more stop: Ewan's office.

The coast appeared to be clear.

She plopped more papers down on his immaculate desk and placed a hand on his state-of-the-art telephone.

"Just what do you think you're doing?"

Jo spun around at the voice.

Ewan stood in the doorway, eyes narrow and deadly.

Jo's blood ran stone cold.

"I'll never be able to enjoy paint by numbers again," Theresa mumbled to herself as she applied a large stroke to the moat of Prince Siegfried's castle.

"What?" Hannah asked, a few feet to her left.

"Nothing," Theresa replied. The fumes and the mundane repetition of her painting duties were just getting to be too much. Theresa was *so* over it. But after a few more strokes Theresa experienced an instant attitude adjustment.

A door slammed. Feet stomped.

Anka had stormed out of her dressing room.

And she was headed *directly* Theresa's way.

"Have either of you seen my purse?" Fake Anka demanded. "It was in my dressing room, but now I can't find it."

Was it Theresa's imagination, or did Anka just put extra emphasis on the words *dressing room*?

Both she and Hannah shook their heads no.

She knows I was in there, Theresa figured. She has to.

"Well, *somebody* must have taken it," Fake Anka hissed, staring down Theresa and Hannah coldly before storming off.

"Somebody forgot to take her happy pill this morning," Hannah said, scowling.

She doesn't know the half of it, Theresa thought.

*   *   *

82

Live and Let Spy

"Uh, Ewan, I'm just dropping off these papers for you," Jo blurted, snatching the papers from his desk and waving them in front of his gorgeous face. "Your assistant wasn't in. . . ."

"What were you doing with the phone?" he asked suspiciously.

"The phone?" she asked, oozing little-girl innocence.

But even under her best wide-eyed gaze Ewan's expression didn't soften. "Yes, the phone," he snapped impatiently.

"I was . . . I was going to leave you a personal voice mail," she purred, turning on her flirtatious charm full force. "And I didn't want to do it from my cubicle—you know, where everybody could hear."

Ewan's expression froze for a moment, then softened. He cocked an eyebrow. "A personal voice mail?"

"Yeah," she replied sweetly. "To see if you wanted to get together sometime after work. I wasn't sure how proper it was because I'm an intern. But I figured it was a great way to learn. You know, I'd just *love* to pick your brain."

Ewan soaked up the attention like a sponge. "Well," he said, smiling, "that can certainly be arranged. In fact, tonight there's this gallery opening downtown. You should join me."

"That sounds great. What time?"

"Seven o'clock," he said, eyes sparkling. "Should be lots of fun."

"Yeah, lots of fun," she said cheerily, both excited and terrified. She'd never forget what had happened to her in London when she got too close to the enemy.

She'd almost lost her life.

Beauty is only skin deep, she reminded herself. That was one lesson she'd never forget.

Knock-knock-knock. Theresa rapped on Fake Anka's door, three times fast.

The door flew open.

"What?" Fake Anka growled.

"Just wondering if you found your purse," Theresa said, doing her best to come off like a Good Samaritan. After Hannah's comment about happy pills, Theresa had given some long, hard thought to the situation. Rather than treat Fake Anka like dirt, Theresa decided the best thing to do was treat her like royalty—be sweet, compliment her, suggest getting together for coffee.

In other words, kiss some serious butt.

After all, the closer she got to this carbon copy, the closer she'd be to finding the original.

"Yes, I did," Fake Anka replied, offering no explanation or apology whatsoever.

"I also wanted to introduce myself," Theresa said, trying her best not to let Fake Anka's cold demeanor affect her attitude. "I'm Tiffany Heileman, a huge fan of yours. I think you're just unbelievable."

"Thank you," Fake Anka said, her icy demeanor melting a half an inch.

"Um, I'd love to get together for coffee sometime

and hear all about your experiences." She paused. "Maybe not."

Fake Anka sized her up for a moment before saying anything. Her expression was as sour as if Theresa had asked her to go on a blind date with the stinky maintenance man.

Theresa was about to turn and leave when Fake Anka finally answered.

"Perhaps . . . we will see."

"Seat fourteen-D—right this way, mate," Caylin told a ballet goer.

She was operating on automatic pilot. Even though her bod was in the theater, Caylin's mind was still on the office and the events from a few hours prior.

When Ottla had amicably agreed to take Caylin on a tour of the under-renovation executive offices, Caylin had thought it would be a piece of cake to ditch Ottla and case the joint out solo.

But that didn't wash. Although Ottla had been happy enough about granting the tour, Ottla had refused to leave Caylin's side. Each of Caylin's attempts at privacy—asking to realphabetize the files, reorganize the paperwork, even offering to clean the place—was immediately shot down.

"No one but authorized personnel is allowed in here without supervision," Ottla had replied, her tone implying Caylin was totally *un*authorized.

Caylin knew then that she would have to break in.

Her inner adrenaline junkie was so thrilled that

even ushering couldn't bring her down. She bounced up the steps two at a time.

"Your tickets, sport?" she called as she rapidly approached an older gentleman with a much younger bleached blond on his arm. Whoa, wait a minute, she thought. The graying hair, the tall, lean frame—where did she know this guy from?

The guy handed her his tickets and smiled confidently, cockily. Of course—Mitchell von Strauss, head of InterCorp!

"Right this way, sir," she said, praying that her recognition didn't show on her face.

As she turned to show them to their seats her brain was buzzing with one big question: *Could they be here to finalize assassination plans?*

As they slid into their seats—first row, center—the bleached blond looked Caylin straight in the eye. "Could you tell me where the ladies' room is?"

Caylin glanced up at the growing group of people at the top of the stairs, all waiting to be shown to their seats. "I was actually headed there myself," she said, deciding to blow off her usherly duties so she could dig for potential dirt. "Let me show you the way."

"This artist is very big here in Prague, apparently," Ewan said as he and Jo strolled into Galerie MXM's small, dark interior.

"I can see why," Jo muttered, checking out the gigantic canvases dominated by wild colors and abstract images.

Live and Let Spy

Good thing I wore black, Jo thought, looking down at her little velvet dress in gratitude. It seemed to be the color of choice for ninety-five percent of the crowd, so she fit right in.

"Maybe we should buy some of his work for the office," Ewan mused. "The Prague office is so bland compared to the American headquarters."

Jo nodded blankly in response. She desperately wanted to change the subject to Anka and the signing. She knew that she had to take it slow, however. Nice and easy.

As Ewan greeted a young, preppy-looking guy Jo soaked in the party atmosphere. Very glam, very Euro, very so-hip-it's-sick crowd. Lots of money in the room, obviously. Tuxedoed waiters offered glasses of champagne too tall to sip and tiny appetizers too beautiful to eat.

"*Rohlik?*" a waiter asked as he offered up a large tray of finger rolls.

"*Dekuji,*" Jo said in gratitude. She popped one into her mouth as Ewan turned to face her.

"An old polo chum," he explained, gesturing toward the departing male figure. "I would have introduced you, but he's quite boring."

"Then I guess I should thank you," she said with a laugh. "Where do you know him from?"

"Switzerland," he said. "Have you ever been?"

"I've been everywhere," she gushed, playing up the "socialite" end of her false identity.

"Oh yes, that's right." He laughed, curiosity obviously piqued. "Around the block a few times, correct?"

"Daddy had wads of money," she gushed. "Anywhere I wanted to go, I went."

"Then what was it that prompted your sky's-the-limit self to come to InterCorp?" he asked, his tone fun and flirtatious. "I'm dying to know."

"Well, although money's been no object throughout my life—well, perhaps *because* of it—I adore nothing more than earning buckets and buckets of it on my very own," she explained. "And I figured the best way to learn how to do this was at InterCorp." She smiled at Ewan coyly. "You are, after all, the experts."

"You definitely came to the right place," Ewan said. "In fact, you'll have the opportunity to rub elbows with every sort of financial mogul at the open-trade-pact signing next week. It's obscene how much cash these people have—almost *insane*."

"Almost," Jo replied with a wink. "Do you know much about the trade pact?"

"Only that it's a pain to even think about," Ewan said. "So enough about the financial world. What are your other passions?"

"There are sooo many," Jo cooed, momentarily bummed that he wasn't giving up any dirt on the signing. "The ballet, of course. I went a few nights ago, and Anka Perdova was amazing. Have you had a chance to see her?"

"She's genius, pure genius," he agreed, looking a tad uncomfortable. "And speaking of genius, the more I look at this art, the more I feel like it's seriously lacking."

88

Live and Let Spy

"I agree, but I didn't want anyone to overhear and think I was a snob."

Ewan smiled. "Would you care to leave?"

Jo hesitated. "Where to?"

"Are you hungry?" he asked, a mischievous glint in his eye.

"Ravenous," she replied. What better place to pick Ewan's brain than at an intimate dinner for two?

"I don't feel like dealing with any crowds right now," he explained. "We could swing by my apartment and order in. That way we can really talk."

Uh-oh.

His apartment?

Jo didn't know what to say. Things were moving awfully fast. If Jo had been on a real first date—and not a secret mission—she would *never* go back to a guy's apartment. It was the baddest of all bad ideas.

Or was it?

She fingered the pea-size lump in the lining of her purse—the phone bug that she didn't get to install in Ewan's office that afternoon. Maybe she could get his home phone. . . .

With a sultry smile she slipped her hand into the crook of his elbow. "Ewan, I thought you'd never ask."

Caylin followed von Strauss's bleached blond friend into the lounge area of the ladies' room. "First time to see this production?" she asked, trying to sound like nothing more than a well-meaning usher.

"No," the woman answered curtly.

"Isn't Anka bloody amazing?" Caylin asked.

"Yes," the woman responded, lowering her gaze before disappearing into the bathroom area.

Did she lower her eyes because she doesn't want to talk to me anymore, Caylin wondered, or because she knows something about the true Anka's whereabouts?

She washed her hands and touched up her lipstick to kill time.

Then she had an idea.

She slipped her hand into her pocket and brought out her bottle of eyedrops. But it held a lot *more* than just eyedrops. In fact, it held exactly what Caylin needed right now.

When the blond emerged to fix her makeup, Caylin was ready.

"My blasted contacts make my eyes bone-dry!" she complained, dropping one, two, then three drops in each eye.

Snap-snap-snap. The miniature camera inside the bottle clicked softly, taking frame after frame while drop after drop hit Caylin's pupils.

The woman again averted her gaze as she made her exit, totally clueless that her bathroom break had just turned into a Kodak moment.

"This place is unbelievable," Jo cooed as she looked around Ewan's obscenely large loft. The chocolate brown couches, cherry-wood furniture, and big-screen TV screamed "boy," but in a tasteful way. However, no framed pics or quirky touches personalized the space. The quarters were so generic, in fact, that the loft could have easily passed for a Pottery Barn showroom. "Not many personal touches, huh?"

He shrugged. "I've only been here a week. But I do have my high school rowing trophy up on the mantel. First place."

She eyed the silver award, unimpressed. Not that she was expecting to find a ransom note for Anka on the refrigerator or anything, but she had hoped she'd find something more juicy than high school memorabilia.

Jo smiled. "I bet you miss your creature comforts from back home."

"Oh yeah."

"Which ones?"

"You know—the dog, the pool, the Lamborghini."

Jo gasped. "The *Lamborghini?*"

"I love it," he said. "But believe me, I'm not complaining. At twenty-four, I couldn't have it much better than this."

Jo fought off the urge to ask for a spec list of the Lam. She was slavering to know all about it . . . but there were more pressing issues at hand.

"Were you a boy genius or something?"

"I think I'll pick the 'or something,'" he said with a laugh. "Would you excuse me for a moment?"

Jo nodded and Ewan left the room. She heard the bathroom door down the hall close.

She breathed a sigh of relief. Now was her chance to bug the phone. She slid her hand into her purse and retrieved the tiny device. Her fingers were shaking so badly that she almost dropped it.

Steady, girl.

Jo hurriedly grabbed his living room phone and inserted the bug in the receiver. But as she was putting the receiver back in position, she heard Ewan enter the room behind her.

"Who are you calling?" he asked.

"Checking my messages," she said, adopting her best panicked expression. "I'm sorry, Ewan, but I'm going to have to take a rain check on dinner. Something's suddenly come up."

"Oh," he replied.

Ewan's sad puppy-dog expression hit Jo right where it hurt—but she knew she had to leave before anything happened, for better or for worse. Still, poor Ewan seemed *sooo* disappointed. It was positively heartbreaking.

"Everything okay, I hope?" Ewan asked.

"Nothing life or death, but I do have to run," she explained.

"Let me drive you," he offered.

"No, I'll grab a cab," she insisted. No way would she let him drive her anywhere near headquarters!

Ewan shot her a quizzical look.

"I need to make several stops," she lied, "and I have no idea how long I'm going to be."

"Well, at least let me walk you out." He grabbed her little faux fur coat and held it out for her.

What a gent, Jo thought, her heart temporarily melting. It quickly froze up again, and not because she was back out on the frigid streets. How could

Ewan be a gent if he was mixed up in a psychotic assassination plot?

I have to do something about these hormones, Jo told herself.

Jo shivered while Ewan hailed her a taxi. "Remind me to never again wear a little black dress in subzero temperatures," she joked, teeth chattering.

"Little black dresses suit you," Ewan replied gently. "Better than power suits, at least from where I'm standing."

A cab pulled up and Jo felt a surge of relief. She was turning into a Popsicle.

As if reading her mind, Ewan attempted to melt Jo with a warm kiss as she slid into the cab.

She turned her cheek just in time.

"Thanks for a lovely evening," she said, shrugging out of his embrace. "I'll see you in the morning."

She slammed the door and the cab pulled away, leaving Ewan behind, sadness and confusion written all over his gorgeous face.

"Can you believe he tried to kiss me?" Jo asked Caylin and Theresa later that evening back in the living room of 3-S. Jo was sprawled out on the oriental rug while Caylin and Theresa lounged on the antique couches. Theresa's homemade mix of French pop blared from the speakers.

"Why is it you always end up with the guy adventures?" Theresa asked.

"Yeah, I'm wondering that myself," Caylin said,

swinging her blond locks over her shoulder. "Absolutely no cute guys work in the theater offices. In fact, it's a *total* no-man's-land."

"Backstage is no boyfest, either," Theresa moaned. "Except . . . well, there is one guy. . . ."

"Really?" Jo asked, perking up.

"Who is he?" Caylin demanded. "We're all on a need-to-know basis, remember?"

Theresa burst out laughing. "Just kidding. He's a maintenance man. And he stinks! You never smelled BO like this! It's like bad cheese or something."

Jo groaned. "Gross!"

"Did you get his number?" Caylin asked.

"Har-dee-har," Theresa said. "He caught me in Anka's dressing room. I thought I was toast. At least Jo's target is cute."

"I know it sounds like I'm lucky," Jo insisted, "but I'm telling you—if this guy's involved with the Anka thing, he's pure pond scum. This was no date, trust me."

"Beats bad BO, that's all I'm saying," Theresa said.

"And taking pictures in bathrooms," Caylin added.

The ringing of the aquarium interrupted them.

"Uncle Sam awaits," Theresa said, reaching for the red button.

"Can't we let the machine get it?" Jo joked.

"I heard that, Jo," Uncle Sam replied, his dark silhouette coming into focus among the fish. "Anything to report?"

"I'll say," Jo began. One by one the Spy Girls

delivered their daily reports. Once they were finished, Uncle Sam said he wanted them to listen to something. "And Jo, I believe you'll find this particularly interesting. The first voice belongs to Mitchell von Strauss. The second, we're unsure about as of yet."

Jo scooted to the edge of her seat as a crackling static sounded, interrupted by a deep male voice:

von Strauss: How is she?
Voice 1: Fine. Sedated.
von Strauss: No one's seen her?
V1: Nobody but me.
von Strauss: No one snooping around?
V1: No.
von Strauss: Keep it that way.
Click.

The Spy Girls glared at one another grimly.

"So this confirms our suspicions," Caylin announced. "It's gotta be the real Anka they're talking about."

"It appears so," Uncle Sam said, voice grave. "Does anyone recognize the other voice? Someone who works at the ballet or InterCorp, perhaps?"

"Nope," the girls chorused glumly.

"Any more ideas about 'Danny Thugs I'?" he asked.

The girls again shared blank looks and shrugged, frustrated. "Nope."

"No more of this 'nope' nonsense," Uncle Sam growled. "There are only four days left. If we don't find the real Anka in time to save the prime minister . . ."

"Boom," Caylin replied softly. "They're dead."

"And so are we," Theresa added.

I am just *too* dedicated," Theresa muttered to herself.

She had arrived at the theater around 5:30 A.M. Thursday morning, before Julius or even the stinky maintenance man made it in. But she wasn't there to get a jump start on retouching the great hall of Prince Siegfried's castle.

As if.

She just wanted some uninterrupted snoop time.

What do we have here? Theresa wondered as she surveyed the props closet. In the corner a tall roll of paper sat propped up against a stack of hatboxes.

It looked like a roll of wrapping paper, only it was beige and yellowed. Yet as Theresa unrolled the paper inch by inch, her smile grew wider and wider.

This was no wrapping paper. These were blueprints of the theater, dated 1988. The year of the last renovation, she remembered, flashing back to what Hannah had told her on Monday.

Theresa felt a surge of excitement. These blueprints could be the map that led her to the real Anka—if she was a prisoner somewhere in the theater, that is.

She studied the map for over an hour, taking in every millimeter of the centuries-old layout.

"Looks like an attic is right above the costume closet," she whispered, running a finger over the aged plans.

That would make a great hiding place. . . .

Theresa rushed to the costume closet to check out the ceiling. Sure enough, there was a thin rope hanging from the rafters that, when pulled, would likely deliver a creaky staircase, like her attic door did back home.

Maybe she'd get lucky.

Theresa reached up on tiptoe for the flimsy rope. Her fingertips grazed the braided twine.

She heard heavy footsteps. And a low whistle.

Theresa gasped. She knew that whistle all too well—Julius!

What was *he* doing in so early?

Theresa frantically rolled up the blueprints and crouched in the corner.

The steps grew louder. The whistling was casual, as if Julius was simply making early morning rounds, finding dozens of imaginary faults in the set designs. For future torture of set painters, no doubt.

The steps paused right outside the door. Theresa held her breath.

What was he looking at?

The whistling stopped.

He'd seen something he didn't like, she knew. Did she leave some trace of her snooping?

Four heartbeats. Five. A dozen.

Finally Julius growled, "Stupid people . . . stupid, stupid, stupid people."

His whistling resumed and the heavy footsteps faded away.

Doesn't Julius ever sleep? Theresa wondered, letting out a sigh. So much for early morning snooping. She'd have to wait until lunch. And even then she knew she might not get much of a chance to see the attic.

Before she gently closed the closet door behind her, she gave the attic door one last searching look.

Please be up there, Anka, she prayed. Just be there.

"No way!" Jo whispered as she approached her cubicle Thursday morning.

In the middle of her desk sat a crystal vase containing a dozen red roses!

Trembling, Jo extracted the attached card from its envelope.

> *Selma,*
>
> *Sorry our evening was cut short. Hope everything turned out okay and that I can honor that rain check you're holding. Free Saturday afternoon?*
>
> *E.*

"Take a chill pill, girl," Jo warned herself. This was actually bad news. She wasn't supposed to get too close.

But what an opportunity to get information!

"You can go . . . but strictly for research," she re-solved, skipping over to Ewan's office to accept his invite.

But when she spied his blond hair, those blue eyes, and that seductive smile through the door-way, she was overwhelmed by one supersize, super-scary realization—

I like him too much already.

Theresa froze. Panic coursed through her veins.

The attic stairs creaked like an old man snoring!

It was lunchtime, and she'd snuck back into the costume closet to take another shot at the attic. But as she tiptoed up the stairs the wood sounded as if it were ready to disintegrate beneath her.

She paused, listening.

Nothing. No Julius, no Hannah.

She continued up, trying to step lightly. No dice. She'd have to risk it.

The attic was musty and damp, and the dim overhead bulb offered little light.

She took a step forward and kicked something. A thick cloud of dust erupted from the floor in front of her—just as she breathed in. A huge poof of soot shot straight into her nose.

She sneezed.

Ah-ah-ah-choooo!

This was no prissy little achoo. Theresa cranked out a whopper that rattled the rafters!

"Oh, man," she grunted, wiping her nose. "I'm dead."

Live and Let Spy

She listened for a reaction from below.

Nothing.

Maybe she got lucky again.

She covered her mouth and nose and peered into the gloom. If Anka was up here, she knew she had company now, that was for sure.

"Anka?" Theresa called out.

She heard movement and froze. Could it be her? "Anka?"

Theresa held her breath in anticipation. But instead of receiving a reply from the missing ballerina, she felt the pressure of little feet scampering over the top of her boot.

She shuddered. In the darkness she could just make out the shape of a giant rat scurrying toward a pile of boxes. Soon she heard a multitude of supersonic squeals.

"That's it," Theresa growled. "I'm outta here."

Theresa scrambled down the ladder and brushed herself off. Then carefully she poked her head out of the costume closet door and checked the hall.

No one.

She sighed and quietly closed the closet door. Slumping against it in frustration, she wondered where in the world the real Anka Perdova could possibly be.

"Rats," she groaned.

"'Danny Thugs I,'" Jo murmured as she wrote the letters down on the place mat. *Thugs* just seemed too obvious to her.

She had found a small, deserted café not far from InterCorp. It looked like a safe enough place to eat, think, and spy at the same time. The café was dark and silent, with only three other customers.

Jo tore the paper place mat into eleven pieces and wrote a letter from "Danny Thugs I" on each piece. On a whim, she shuffled the letters around. But the more she reorganized the letters, the more she thought her exercise wasn't much more than a way to pass the time until her food arrived.

But still . . . it could've been a code.

She mixed up the letters faster.

The first combination she came up with was *thin gun days.*

"What's that supposed to be?" she muttered under her breath. A .44 trying to slim down to a .38?

An overweight waitress set a chicken sandwich before her, but Jo was too engrossed in her jumble to look up.

Shun Indy tag.

Unfortunately the Indy 500 was months away, and she doubted that Prime Minister Karkovic would be attending.

Duh Ginny sat.

"More like 'duh, Jo, this is pointless,'" she murmured.

Then Jo paused.

Could that be it . . . ?

She organized the letters one final time and smiled.

"Sunday night!" she exclaimed.

Live and Let Spy

The night the assassination was supposed to take place!

Jo congratulated herself . . . on figuring out a piece of information that everyone knew already.

Her heart immediately sank. Suddenly she wasn't so hungry anymore.

"Am I glad to see you!" Caylin whispered as Theresa entered the theater bathroom after lunch.

Caylin grabbed Theresa's arm and pulled her into the nearest stall.

"Can I wash my hands before you abduct me?" Theresa pleaded. "You don't wanna know where they've been."

"Not a chance," Caylin replied. "You have no idea what I've gone through this morning. I've tried everything. Begging, conning, lying. But Ottla will *not* let me into those executive offices!" She kicked the side of the stall. "Got any ideas?"

"How about my key ring?" Theresa whispered, fishing it out of her pocket. "That's how I got into you-know-who's dressing room."

Caylin hefted the key. "That's great, but what about the guard by the door?" she queried. "If he sees me—*bam*, cover blown."

Theresa rubbed her chin, then smiled. "I got it," she replied. "I'll ask the guard to come help me with something onstage. Then you slip right in."

Caylin returned a sly grin and wiggled her eyebrows. "Rock and roll, Spy Girl!"

*   *   *

Moments later Operation Distraction began.

"Sir, could you help me?" Theresa asked the unsmiling guard while Caylin crouched around the corner.

"No glop da English," he said, scowling.

Theresa smiled wanly. "Great. Where's Jo when I need her? Um, let's see. Could. You. Help. Me?"

"No glop da English," the guard repeated, more forcefully.

Theresa motioned him closer. When he leaned in, she took him by the arm and pulled.

"Please," she said in a timid, helpless voice. *"Por favor? Bitte?"*

"Bitte?" the guard asked, brow furrowed.

"Um, *ja!*" she piped. *"Bitte* give me a hand over here, okay?"

No response.

Theresa pulled on the man's arm. He took a step forward.

"Ja! Ja! Attaboy! *Bitte* help! With me. Over here. *Ja!"*

I feel like an idiot, Theresa thought. She *had* to get some language lessons from Jo, if only to avoid looking—and sounding—this stupid in the future.

But the guard actually followed her to the stage.

"I hope you don't freak when you realize I'm lying to you," she muttered to the man. She chanced a glance over her shoulder to make sure Caylin had made it through the locked door. *Bingo.* "Um . . . have you ever actually *used* that gun?"

"No glop da English."

"That's what I thought."

*   *   *

104

Live and Let Spy

Caylin slid the magic key in the door. After a few jiggles it popped open.

Once inside, she warily eyed the black filing cabinets lining the room. Six sprawling wooden desks were weighed down with books and documents, and several cheap prints of ballerinas hung crooked on the yellowed walls. The smell of old papers and dust hung in the air.

Caylin darted directly to the nearest filing cabinet and began flying through the manila folders, frantically searching for *Anka Perdova* or any name she didn't recognize.

There was nothing in *A*.

She immediately went for *P.*

She paged through the folders one by one. But nothing jumped out. She glanced at her watch. Three minutes had passed.

"Too much time," she whispered. "Come *on.*"

She flipped through even faster, knowing she'd probably miss something. But she couldn't take the chance.

She neared the back of the *P* drawer and started thinking which letter to tackle next.

Then she saw it.

A file marked *Alexandra Parsons.*

Caylin knew there was no such person in the ballet troupe. But she could've been anyone, an employee of InterCorp, a dancer long since gone.

She opened the file, anyway. It was the only name that was even close.

"Alexandra Parsons," she read. She looked

over the dancer's vitals and felt a surge of excitement. They matched Anka Perdova's. Exactly. Which meant that they would match the imposter's, too.

"This has gotta be her," Caylin reasoned. "It's just gotta be!"

The doorknob rattled.

Caylin's heart jumped into her throat. Was it Theresa? Or that security guard?

Caylin dove under the nearest desk.

The door creaked open.

"Muriel?" Ottla called. "Are you in here?"

Caylin held her breath, praying Ottla wouldn't actually come in.

"Muriel?" Her voice was closer now. "Muriel?"

Caylin's heart pounded. Her hands shook so badly that she had to ball them into fists.

Get out of here, Ottla, Caylin silently commanded. Give it up.

After a few seconds Ottla's footsteps retreated and the door slammed.

Caylin sighed in relief. She waited a few moments and pulled herself up from beneath the desk. She slipped the file underneath her sweater. As she snuck out of the office Caylin crossed her fingers tightly, praying that she finally got her mitts on the money.

"The letters in 'Danny Thugs I' spell out 'Sunday night,'" Jo reported to Uncle Sam on her cell phone on her way back to the office. Her eyes darted all around her to ensure that no one from the office was on the sidewalk nearby.

"Well done, Jo," Uncle Sam proclaimed. "I'm glad you called because I want you to hear this call that came in late last night. The first voice is Ewan's. We don't know who the woman is yet."

The word *Ewan* was enough to spur Jo's interest. As a large truck rumbled past, Jo stuck her finger in her right ear in order to hear better.

Ewan: Hello?
Woman: Ewan, you are such a snake!
Ewan: What? What'd I do?
Woman: You went to the gallery opening with some bimbo, that's what! I saw her! Who was she?
Ewan: Just a girl from the office—she's nobody.
Woman: Nobody—yeah, right. I'm coming over.
Ewan (sighing loudly): I'll be downstairs.
Click.

"A *bimbo?*" Jo exclaimed. "A *nobody?* That creep show was lucky I even went to the gallery with him!"

"Hey!" Uncle Sam barked. "Keep your ego out of this, Jo. This mission is about stopping the assassination, not finding Mr. Right."

But Jo couldn't help it. She was so angry, she had to fight back bitter tears.

"Do you understand?"

"Yes," Jo replied stiffly.

"Fine, then. Do you have any idea who the woman is on the tape?"

Jo took a deep breath. "No," she said. "Obviously she's a jealous girlfriend, but I had no clue he was seeing anybody. I mean, he actually asked me out again for Saturday! The two-timing pig!"

"Any female pictures in his loft?" Sam asked.

"No," Jo replied. "And believe me, I was looking."

"She might know something about Anka's whereabouts," Uncle Sam said, his voice cutting out for a second. "Can you hold?"

While waiting for Uncle Sam to return to the line, Jo looked at InterCorp's building looming in the distance. Who wanted to go back to work when "Danny Thugs I" was meaningless and Ewan had a girlfriend that she—his prime investigator—didn't even know *existed*?

"Theresa and Caylin are conferencing on the other line," Uncle Sam stated. "So I'll talk to you tonight. Keep your eyes and ears peeled for any information on Ewan's girlfriend."

Jo hit "end" and scowled. Despite her nausea, she felt more determined than ever to go out and get the goods.

Nobody called her a nobody and got away with it. *Nobody.*

"This is great work," Uncle Sam told Caylin and Theresa, who were conferencing him from two separate cell phones. Caylin was perched on a park bench near the theater while Theresa stood in front of an apartment building two blocks over.

"Alexandra Parsons, Anka Perdova—A.P.,"

Uncle Sam continued. "An unusual coincidence. Perhaps this Ms. Parsons is the imposter in this scenario. But you had better FedEx the folder to me right now—there's a drop box three blocks north of the theater. Don't keep that information on you for longer than you have to."

"Got it." Caylin nodded, scanning the passersby to make sure no familiar faces spotted her. Most everyone was distracted by a marionette puppet show in the park; they didn't even give her a second glance.

"Should I snag those blueprints, too?" Theresa asked.

"Definitely," Uncle Sam replied. "You need to know that theater like it's your bedroom. And by the way, the ID on the pictures you shot of von Strauss's escort came back, Caylin. It's his daughter."

"His daughter?" Caylin echoed, aghast. "Oh, drag. That's so *non*juicy."

"Afraid so," he said. "And knowing von Strauss's attitude toward his family, he would probably never put his own daughter in danger. It's unlikely she knows anything."

"Great," Caylin muttered, slumping against the park bench. "Another dead end."

"Want to go grab some joe?" Hannah asked Theresa after a grueling evening performance. The backstage area swarmed with dancers and technical people preparing to go home for the night.

Theresa had her eye on one superstar dancer in particular.

"Nah, I have to get going," Theresa said as she watched Fake Anka gather her bag and coat. "Rain check?"

"Sounds good. Catch you tomorrow."

"Every day," Theresa replied.

As she followed Fake Anka to the exit Theresa slipped a black cap on her head and tucked her tousled brown hair up under it. Her heavy black wool overcoat completed the ensemble.

"So long, Anka!" a dancer said as Fake Anka pushed open the door.

"Uh-huh," the imposter replied gruffly.

Theresa followed her out, lagging about twenty paces behind her.

"Time to find out who you really are," she whispered. She slipped on a pair of sunglasses just to be safe. Even though the sky was dark, she didn't want to chance being recognized. Besides, the lenses were dark enough to shield her eyes but light enough to see out of at night. The perfect stalking shades.

The night air was frigid. Anka headed down the back alley behind the theater toward the main street. Live jazz poured out from an open tavern door, but otherwise the streets were silent. A trio of cats scurried near a bank of trash cans, scavenging for food.

A trash can lid spun from beneath a cat's paws and clattered to the street.

Theresa gasped and ducked behind the cans.

Fake Anka whirled, staring.

Just the cats, just the cats, just the cats, Theresa silently prayed. Keep going!

Live and Let Spy

Moments passed. Fake Anka stared out into the darkness.

One of the stray cats sniffed at Theresa's foot. She gave it a nudge toward the middle of the alley.

The cat meowed loudly and scurried away.

"Just a cat," Theresa whispered, hoping somehow that that would convince Anka.

It did. The imposter turned and continued on. Theresa slipped out from behind the cans and followed.

Anka turned the corner and marched down the street away from the theater. Theresa was careful not to get too close. In fact, Anka was walking almost too fast to keep up with.

"Man, she's in good shape," she huffed.

Then Theresa heard more footsteps.

Only this time they were *behind* her.

The hair on the back of her neck stood on end. Her stomach tightened, and she fought the urge to turn around.

The footsteps got closer while Anka moved farther away.

It didn't matter. Theresa had to look. Just had to. The tingling sensation at her back was almost too much to bear. She gulped and began a count.

One . . .

The steps quickened.

Two . . .

Two's good enough!

Theresa spun around. She saw a burly figure plunge into a shadowy alley, and her whole body went numb with fear.

"I'm outta here," she whispered, running to the left.

There—the tram station! She could lose him there! It was only two blocks away.

Could she make it? She knew she wasn't exactly Caylin in an all-out sprint.

She didn't have time to care.

She took off full tilt. Panic gripped her when she heard pounding footsteps behind her. Then she spotted the tram already at the station—preparing for departure!

No!

Theresa slipped a sweaty palm into her coat pocket and pulled out a tram token as she ran.

She had to time this perfectly. If that tram left . . .

She reached the turnstiles and fumbled with the token and the slot. She didn't look behind her—she didn't want to know.

"Come on, come on!"

The token slipped into the slot. The turnstile gave.

Theresa plunged through and jumped onto the tram just as the doors slid shut.

"All right!" she exclaimed, struggling for breath.

As the tram pulled out she searched around for the burly guy through the window.

She saw nothing.

Who could be following me? she wondered with a shiver as the train accelerated into the cold, dark night.

*　　*　　*

Live and Let Spy

Back at 3-S, Caylin brought a bowl of popcorn to Jo's bedroom. "Look at the bright side, T.," she said. "At least you got away."

Theresa, sprawled next to Jo on her enormous canopy bed, smiled. "Very funny," she replied. "That dude was *huge*."

"You got a good look at him?" Jo asked excitedly.

"N-No," she stammered. "I could just tell. He was *huge*, that's all. No other distinguishing characteristics. Sorry."

"Intense," Caylin said. "Well, now that we found this weird Alexandra Parsons file, maybe we can get this sucker solved."

"Alexandra Parsons, huh?" Theresa said. "Think that's the imposter?"

Caylin shrugged. "Looks that way to me. But I guess we'll soon find out."

Jo took a handful of popcorn. "And at least we don't have to waste any more time on 'Danny Thugs I.'"

"Speaking of not wasting any more time," Caylin replied. "Aren't you glad you didn't waste any more time on Ewan?"

Jo rolled her eyes. "The freak. Calling me a nobody. *Me!*"

"Oh, the humanity!" Theresa cried dramatically.

"Oh, the *humility*," Caylin deadpanned.

Jo sported a smile as wide and evil as Godzilla's. "Yeah, well, freak-boy Ewan is about to find out how much damage a nobody can do!"

"**C**ome out, come out, wherever you are!" Jo whispered as she scoped out InterCorp's halls for any suspicious-looking areas on Friday morning. Since Anka could be hidden *anywhere*—not just at the theater—Jo was making it her business to go over every square inch of the building with a fine-tooth comb.

As Jo approached a door marked Supplies she put her hand on its metal knob. A secretary in high heels clicked by, and Jo gave her a wave and a smile.

Once the woman passed, Jo tried the door again. Locked.

She used the magic key, and abracadabra, she was in.

"I have to get one of these," she whispered.

Jo scanned the room. Although there was no Anka to be found, there were no supplies to be found, either. The closet was filled ceiling high with boxes marked Confidential and IRS.

"Wow," she mused. "Heavy-duty. Pay dirt, perhaps?"

She snapped some quick mascara pix of the boxes and bolted back to her cubicle before her boss could notice she was even gone. Once she got back and checked her e-mail, she was thrilled to find that Gottwald would be in a meeting for the next hour.

A whole hour.

Cool.

"Time to see what's in my boss's office," she sang under her breath.

Confidently striding into Gottwald's office with a packet of papers under her arm, Jo operated as if she had every right to be there. Who was going to say anything? She *was* his acting assistant.

Von Strauss's assistant poked her head into the office moments later. "Can I help you?"

Jo jumped in surprise. "Uh, just looking for a folder Mr. Gottwald needs. You know, for his meeting."

The woman nodded slowly. "I see."

"I'll let you know if I need anything, thanks," Jo said sweetly, shooting her a confident smile.

But after searching Gottwald's files for the next half hour, Jo was feeling anything *but* confident.

She found nothing.

Then she paused. She caught a flash of red poking out from under his computer keyboard. She lifted the keyboard.

A red folder marked Trade Pact. Right there. Hidden away.

Jackpot! Jo thought triumphantly.

Holding her breath, she opened the folder. It held only one piece of paper. But it was worth a thousand words. It was a confidential memo about the financial loss that InterCorp would suffer if the open-trade pact was signed!

Millions! Zillions! Enough to start another country in a really good neighborhood!

Immediately she ran the paper through Gottwald's personal fax machine and made a copy. Then she placed the original back in its folder under the keyboard. All before Gottwald even returned, she thought smugly as she slid into her cubicle and stuck the photocopy in her Gucci briefcase for safekeeping.

"Whatcha got there, Selma?" came a voice.

Jo whirled and saw Ewan. She clicked her briefcase shut and forced herself to smile.

"Just a copy of an article I found interesting," she said automatically, shifting into flirt mode. "On money. My favorite subject."

"Really?" he asked, eyes narrowing. "What about money?"

Did he see me in Gottwald's office? she wondered.

No. She was just being paranoid.

"Best buys at Tiffany's," she quipped. "My first stop on my next jaunt to New York."

As Ewan looked into her eyes and smiled Jo felt just like Audrey Hepburn in Tiffany's—*Breakfast at,* that is. Like the smartest, most glamorous girl in the world!

As Theresa approached her locker she first saw a flash of white, then a bloodred psychotic scrawl.

What was it . . . a postcard. Taped to her cubby.

117

Her pulse raced. Who could it be from? she wondered, moving closer.

"*Pozor!*" it read in gigantic crimson letters. An army of foreign words had been scrawled in a madman's slanted script beneath it.

"Uh-oh," she muttered.

She slipped her minitranslator from her coat pocket and punched in the magic word.

Her blood ran cold.

Danger.

She quickly punched in the rest of the words from the postcard and wrote down their English translations one by one. When she'd deciphered the last syllable, her blood positively froze.

Stop snooping into things that are none of your business—or every one of you will die!

"Everyone's dashing about like maniacs today," Ottla told Caylin as the office staff ran through the halls. "Two days until this pact signing, and you'd think the world was coming to an end."

Caylin laughed. "Everyone's gone troppo!"

Ottla gave her a blank look.

"Troppo," she repeated. "Aussie for 'crazy in the head.'"

"Right. Troppo," Ottla said. "Listen, Muriel, we need each department head to sign off on this." Ottla handed Caylin an interoffice memo outlining each department's responsibilities for Sunday. "This will take some legwork on your part," she continued, "but it needs to be done today."

118

Live and Let Spy

"No problem," Caylin said, secretly thrilled to be able to snoopify some more. Even though Theresa had covered practically every inch of the place and found no Anka, Caylin was dying to take a crack at it herself.

After scoring Theresa's boss's signature and calling "Cheerio!" to her fellow Spy Girl, Caylin walked down the hall toward the head choreographer's office. En route she stopped short in front of what looked like a small utility closet.

Caylin regarded it with fascination. She had never even noticed it before. Seeing as how a simple utility closet had borne one of the most important pieces of evidence in the London mission, she was just itching to have a look inside.

"Wonder what's behind door number one?" Caylin whispered as she opened the unlocked door and entered the damp, musty interior. As Caylin reached out a hand to feel for a light switch the door slammed behind her.

"Uh-oh," Caylin moaned.

The closet was totally black. Caylin blindly groped for the doorknob. It wouldn't budge.

"Uh-oh squared."

A twinge of panic crept into Caylin's stomach. She was trapped. And she didn't even have her cell phone on her to beep Theresa!

As reality hit, Caylin dropped her clipboard with a clatter and sank to her khaki-covered knees. She felt as if the walls were closing in on her already.

Claustrophobia—Caylin's worst enemy.

"Somebody help!" she yelled, kicking the door.

She blindly ran her hands along the door, searching for anything. But there was no keyhole, and the hinges were on the outside.

The only things she could find were a broom, a mop and bucket, and a fuse box on the wall.

Trapped.

Claustrophobia.

She forced herself not to think about it. She kicked the door again. But she couldn't help it. The walls were too close. She could smother, or be crushed, or the roof could collapse, the theater was so old. . . .

No!

Caylin took a deep breath and thought of snowy slopes, the wind in her hair, and her snowboard. It didn't help. The irrational fear gripped her tight. Her tumultuous tummy turned somersault after somersault.

Will anyone ever find me? she wondered with another aggravated kick.

And how would she explain herself if someone did?

Doubts and insecurities slam-danced around Caylin's brain as she tried to come up with a game plan.

Don't bother, you're nailed, they'll catch you and they'll kill you. . . .

"Shut up!" she commanded the taunting voices in her mind. She finally hit her forehead against the door in frustration.

Live and Let Spy

"So we solved our last mission—so what," Caylin said bitterly. "The conference is in forty-eight hours, we still don't have one solid lead, and I'm stuck in a freaking closet!"

Ugh, I sound like a whiny brat! she thought, disgusted with herself. Caylin had always been a fighter. She was *not* one to give up. And she wasn't about to start now.

Self-pity abruptly transformed into unqualified rage.

She pounded on the door with unprecedented force. "Let me outta here!" she snarled, a caged animal.

After a few minutes of her furious pounding, the knob finally jiggled.

Relief flooded through Caylin's veins. Finally!

The door swung wide and she was met with a stench so thick, she could taste it.

"*Ano?*" a maintenance man asked in bewilderment.

Caylin squinted as the hall light blinded her.

"Ugh!" she replied, covering her nose in disgust.

"*Ano?*" he asked again.

"*Nemluvím cesky!*" Caylin immediately said. Translation: "I don't speak Czech!"

She scooped up her clipboard and slipped past him. "So much for a breath of fresh air," she added.

And so much for finding any more leads.

Let's see you thugs follow me now! Theresa silently dared as she strolled to Fake Anka's dorm on Friday afternoon.

Theresa had asked Julius if she could knock off at

121

lunch, pleading that good ol' "time of the month" crampage. When Julius surprisingly obliged her request, she pulled her hair into a messy bun, donned some sunglasses, and hit the door double quick before he had a chance to change his mind.

She clutched the magic key ring in her pocket.

"Identification, please," the dorm security guard requested as soon as Theresa entered the lobby.

Without so much as glancing up, Theresa flashed the man her theater ID and rushed past him, beelining straight for the dormitory directory.

About eight lines down she hit pay dirt: *Anka Perdova—5-E.*

Theresa scurried up the stairs, taking them two at a time.

"Here goes nothing," she muttered to herself as 5-E came within sight.

She slipped her magic key into the doorknob. "Open, sesame," she whispered, her heart filled with high expectations over the possible treasures hiding behind it. It swung open easily.

She stepped in.

An ear-piercing wail sounded, and Theresa panicked.

A burglar alarm!

Theresa spotted the beaten-up plastic keypad next to the door. It was loose on its screws.

Defuse it! she told herself.

The plastic cover came off in her hand. The wires underneath were old and frayed. One of them snapped in her hand, but the alarm continued to shriek.

Too much time . . .

The phone rang.

That was the last straw.

Theresa bolted. She slammed Anka's door shut and ran toward the fire door at the end of the hall. She heard the creak of a door opening behind her, but she didn't care. She whipped open the fire door and dashed through it, finding herself on the fire escape. Anka's alarm wailed on and on inside.

Scrambling down the stairs, Theresa gasped as she nearly slipped on the icy metal.

Don't look down, she told herself, white knuckling the freezing rails for dear life. Five floors was a long way down.

She frantically descended the steps one by one. Her hands were freezing on the steel rails. Bizarre thoughts bombarded her brain: Would she be caught? Did Fake Anka know her identity? Was the mission blown?

Finally she made it to solid ground.

Theresa ducked into the nearest alley and peered back at the dorm.

Seconds later the security guard burst out of the dormitory doors, screaming incomprehensibly at the top of his lungs.

Theresa sighed. Now what? She needed to do something. Waiting around for the police to catch her was *not* an option.

Her gaze fell upon a hotel across the street from the dorm.

Theresa smiled.

"I need, um . . ." Theresa looked down at her pocket translator. "I need . . . *pokoj do ulice . . . na jih . . . poschodi . . . pet*," she told the hotel clerk in pidgin Czech. "A room facing the street on the fifth floor, south side," she followed up.

"Four thousand crowns," the overweight clerk said without looking up.

Theresa passed the woman her Visa, emblazoned with the name Camilla Stevens—a popular Tower alias.

The woman tossed her a key. The key was stamped with the number 555.

The magic key probably would have done the trick on the hotel room door, Theresa figured. But with the luck she was having that day, she'd probably walk in on two newlyweds.

As soon as she entered 555 Theresa marched to the window and jerked open the curtains.

"Yes!"

She had, as planned, a direct view of Anka's room.

"Let's zoom in," she said, digging around in her pockets for the opera glasses she sometimes used to check out the last act of the ballet from the balcony.

She caught sight of the security guard conferring with two Prague police officers. After a few moments they shut Anka's door and left.

The apartment sat empty.

Live and Let Spy

"Guess there's nothing to do now but wait," Theresa muttered. She took a deep breath and flipped on the TV. The fact that there were only four stations to choose from didn't matter much.

Theresa couldn't understand a word anyone was saying, anyway.

Just as she was about to nod off from boredom, Theresa saw an overhead light go on over at Anka's.

"Gotcha!" Theresa cheered. Squinting, she saw two blurry figures enter the room. Pulse racing, she hopped up from the bed and scrambled for her opera glasses to get a better look at Fake Anka's companion.

"Who's your boyfriend?" she whispered into the darkness, bringing the glasses to her eyes. As the fuzzy figures came into focus Theresa gasped at the man standing just inches away from Fake Anka.

Ewan!

They were arguing. They paced back and forth, their gestures angry and wild. Ewan raised his hand above his head and Theresa winced and closed her eyes, bracing herself for the blow.

But when she opened her lids, Ewan was giving Fake Anka a deep, passionate kiss.

Theresa's opera glasses hit the floor with a resounding clunk.

"I just can't believe they're a couple!" Jo cried back at 3-S. "So *she* was the one Uncle Sam got on tape!"

"Looks that way," Theresa replied.

The speaker phone rang in the living room. Caylin immediately dove for it.

"Yo," she said.

"Hello, my superfly spies," came Danielle's voice. "Good news."

"We like good news," Caylin said, rubbing Jo's back consolingly.

"I've located Anka Perdova's family."

"Really? Where, in Moscow or something?" Jo asked.

"In Ohio."

"*Ohio?*" Theresa echoed, confused. "Whoa. I'm missing something."

"Yeah . . . we *all* were missing something," Caylin said, a smile creeping across her face. "Don't you get it? Alexandra Parsons *isn't* the imposter. She's the real deal."

Theresa gasped. "You mean—"

"Yes!" Caylin cried. "Alexandra Parsons is actually Anka Perdova! Right, Danielle?"

"Yes sirree," Danielle confirmed. "I guess it's some big secret of hers. Her mother is of Russian descent, but our Anka is baseball and apple pie all the way."

Jo gasped. "So she's been fooling everybody all this time? No way!"

"Affirmative," Danielle replied.

"She's a darned convincing Russian," Caylin exclaimed.

"We're talking Academy Award here," Danielle

126

said. "Apparently *everyone* was duped. I'm guessing that only the higher-ups at the New Russian Ballet are in on it—hence the lengths you had to go through to nab this folder. Who knows, maybe Alexandra thought she'd have a better shot at the NRB if she pretended to be Russian."

"Maybe it was her *only* shot," Caylin suggested.

"Exactly," Danielle agreed. "And maybe the execs finally found out her secret, so they're covering it up to save face."

Theresa took a deep breath. "It's just so hard to believe. . . ."

"And get this," Danielle said. "I paid her folks a visit, posing as a reporter. They said they haven't talked to her in a week and a half. And interestingly enough, they received a postcard from her just yesterday. I palmed it and e-mailed you a color scan."

"Danielle," Jo teased, "you sneak."

Theresa darted to fetch her laptop, then signed on. Within a matter of seconds she was staring at a downloaded file of the postcard.

"The handwriting's pretty shaky," Theresa noted.

"And she usually writes in a very neat script, according to Mama," Danielle said. "Okay—postmark Prague, three days ago. Read along with me here and see what you think.

> *Hi, everyone, I'm fine but very busy. You know I'm not one to whine or anything, but things have been really hectic and I'm beat.*

127

Can't wait to see you on holiday.
Cheers,
Alex

"It sounds generic enough," Caylin said.

"What about the front of the postcard?" Jo suggested, staring at the screen intently. "Could you zap that over?"

"Sure thing," Danielle said. Her scanner buzzed in the background. A few seconds later the file appeared in Theresa's incoming mailbox.

The card featured a shot of a child ballerina with daisies in her hair.

"Magnify that." Jo brought her nose closer to the screen while Theresa blew up the image four hundred percent.

"What are those little splatters in the right-hand corner?" Jo asked, referring to five or six spots on the image. "Is that just on the scan or on the original?"

Danielle paused. "Good eye, Jo—I didn't even notice those. It's definitely on the card. It's something red."

The Spy Girls shared fearful glances.

"Blood?" Caylin wondered grimly.

"I'll have forensics check it out," Danielle promised.

"Does the card have a smell?" Jo asked.

"A smell?" Danielle repeated. "Actually, it's kind of musty. Dank."

"Strange," Jo murmured.

128

Live and Let Spy

"I just hope this means the real Anka is still alive," Theresa said, sighing deeply.

"Yeah." Caylin ran a hand anxiously through her blond hair. "But if we don't get on the stick, she may not be for much longer."

"And neither will Karkovic," Jo added.

Theresa shook her head. "Let's face it. We're all doomed."

At least my heart doesn't skip a beat when I see him anymore, Jo thought as she looked into Ewan's eyes Saturday afternoon.

They were brunching at Luna, a hip eatery with fresh-cut flowers on the tables, colorful murals on the walls, and candles everywhere. Despite the Fake Anka revelation, Uncle Sam had told Jo to keep the brunch date and use the opportunity to pump Ewan for information. Although Ewan hadn't yet revealed anything over pancakes, Jo remained optimistic.

At some point the guy's got to slip, she resolved, leaning back in her seat and smiling wickedly. And when he did, she'd be right there to nail him.

"Are you excited about the ballet tomorrow night?" Jo asked, pulling up the sleeves on her black sweater.

Ewan's face paled so much, his skin looked lighter than his cream thermal. "The ballet?" he repeated with a gulp. "I guess so, but I'm more interested in the trade pact. For me the ballet is simply an appetizer to the main course."

"But Anka is just amazing," Jo exclaimed. "I can't wait to see her in action again."

"She is quite something," Ewan agreed. "It will be a lot of fun, I suppose."

"So what are you going to do now?" Jo asked, hoping she could score an invite to hang out with him for a bit longer.

"You wouldn't believe it if I told you," he said with a twinkle in his eye.

She grinned. Thirty-thousand watts. "Try me."

"You'll probably think it's stupid," he said, averting his gaze.

"I promise I won't laugh," she replied.

He paused. "Well, I'm actually taking a skydiving lesson. At two."

"Sk-skydiving?" Jo echoed. Although she loved flying down the freeway, free falling from ten thousand feet was an entirely different story.

"I'm trying to conquer my fear of flying," he confessed.

"By jumping out of a plane?"

He shrugged. "They say it works. Want to come with me?"

Jo hesitated.

Skydiving. Jumping out of a perfectly good airplane.

Should she put herself in danger to score some juicy details or stay on solid ground and possibly miss out?

"I'd love to," Jo finally replied, hoping she wasn't making a big, big mistake.

"Jeez, for an international imposter and potential murderess, your Saturday sure is a snoozer,"

Live and Let Spy

Theresa muttered as she watched Fake Anka exit a grocery store from a hundred feet back. Since the theater was closed to stage staff and dancers for pact-signing preparations, Theresa had spent the better part of her morning trailing the deadly diva.

So far it'd been one big laugh riot—the laundry, the gym, now the grocery store. What's next, the post office? Theresa wondered, taken aback by the fact that such a devious supercriminal could lead such a boring existence.

Theresa had been hoping to witness secret meetings, hidden hideaways, bang-'em-up car chases—*something* to revive the mission. But no such luck.

When she saw Fake Anka look around suspiciously and jump into a taxi, Theresa practically had a heart attack. Finally—a sign of life!

"Follow that cab," Theresa told a driver as she hopped into his taxi. "And step on it."

Ha! She'd always wanted to say that!

As they trailed Fake Anka's taxi over long, winding roads and across baroque bridges Theresa's interest grew with each mile. And her curiosity level went off the Richter scale when she observed Fake Anka's vehicle stopping in front of what appeared to be a neighborhood carnival, complete with rides, tents, and the whole nine.

"Guess it's time to get on the merry-go-round," Theresa mused.

"When the queen of England arrives, you curtsy," said Ms. Pontiva, the woman Ottla had hired to train the ushers and office staff on how to properly address government officials and royalty. All the tables had been pushed to the corner of the ballroom to give Pontiva enough space to work her magic.

Although Ms. Pontiva was very thorough, Caylin was having a hard time keeping the different customs straight. Such a hodgepodge of countries would be represented! The fact that the importance of this stuff faded in comparison to that of her mission didn't exactly boost her concentration level.

"What happens if we get confused?" she asked, looking up from her notebook.

"Just stay calm," Ms. Pontiva instructed, "and everything will be all right."

"Easy for you to say," Caylin mumbled to herself. "Miss Priss."

Then she froze. Ottla had just entered the theater.

She was accompanied by Prime Minister Karkovic!

Caylin's heart pounded as she laid eyes on the man she'd been sent to protect.

"Excuse me," Ottla said, "but I'd like you to meet Gogol Karkovic, the prime minister of Varokhastan."

With a nervous smile Caylin stuck out her arm to offer a firm handshake. A few other ushers followed suit while one bowed and another curtsied.

"We're still working out our greetings," Ms. Pontiva apologized with a laugh. "Welcome to Prague, Prime Minister."

"Yes, welcome," the group sang while Karkovic smiled ear to ear.

"G'day," Caylin called.

"Your theater is utterly breathtaking," he declared in a strong accent. "I am very pleased to sign pact that will have such enormous influence on our countries."

His aides quickly ushered Karkovic away, noting that his schedule was tight.

Caylin smiled as he said his good-byes. Even a few goose bumps dotted her flesh. He seemed to be such a good man.

Then her smile vanished. That good man had only twenty-four more hours to live.

Not if Caylin could help it. Now that she had met the man in the flesh, she was more determined than ever to keep him from harm's way.

"Okay, I understand," Ewan said into the Airfone. He sat perched in the second row of the eight-seat InterCorp jet. The blue seats were made of plush velvet, and the phone was state-of-the-art.

In the five minutes he'd been on the phone, Jo had been staring out the window, lost in thought.

Anka was somewhere in that world down there, she reflected. But where? How much did she know? Who else was with her?

When he hung up abruptly, Jo noticed Ewan had a strange look on his face.

"Everything okay?" she asked, secretly wondering if the call was about Anka, or Alexandra, or Fake Anka, or . . . whoever.

"Fine," he said, his expression indicating otherwise.

As he looked deep into her eyes she felt a shiver up her spine.

His eyes were cold, vacant.

"What?" she asked in alarm.

He shook his head. "It's nothing, really," he insisted, slapping a plastic smile on his face. "Let's get those parachutes on and get this show on the road."

As Ewan handed her a parachute pack and took one for himself Jo couldn't shake her uneasy feeling. For a terrifying moment she wondered if the parachute Ewan had given her was operable.

"Don't we have an instructor?" Jo asked.

Ewan shook his head. "I know all I need to know."

"Then could you ask the pilot if he can descend a few feet to relieve some of the pressure? My eardrums are about to burst!"

Ewan shot her a strange look before dropping his parachute on the seat and heading up to the cockpit.

While he did, Jo switched her parachute with his. Just in case.

"He's descending to fourteen thousand feet for the jump now," Ewan announced. "Let's get into our gear, shall we?"

"Sure," Jo said, trying to sound brave. But she strapped herself in with shaking hands.

When Ewan studied his pack before putting it on, Jo panicked. Did he realize she made the switch?

"You know how you're always saying you love how Anka dances?" Ewan asked in an overly nonchalant tone as he adjusted the pack on his back.

"Yeah?"

Live and Let Spy

"I was wondering why you mention her so much."

"What do you mean?" she asked. She secured her buckles, not meeting his gaze.

"Look, I *know*, okay?" he spat, his voice getting lower.

"You know what?" Jo asked, her mind spinning. That I'm a Spy Girl, she mused, or that I know he's dating Anka, or that I know Anka's an imposter, or that I know he plans to kill Karkovic?

"That you're living with someone who's been trailing Anka," he said accusingly.

"What?"

"And I know you copied the trade-pact memo," he grumbled. "Whatever it is you're after . . . you won't get it!"

The low, angry note in his voice triggered a memory—the taped phone conversation with von Strauss! It was *Ewan's* voice all along! He really was in on it!

Jo gasped. "You're the guy who—"

Before she could finish her sentence, Ewan lunged for her. Putting her self-defense training into play, she tried to use Ewan's momentum to roll backward and throw him over her. But the fat parachute on her back prevented the move.

They both hit the floor with a thud.

"Let me go!" she screamed, rolling to the side.

"Not on your life," he growled. He pulled her back and pinned her to the ground. "Prague is beautiful from this height. We'll jump together, Selma. You'll just love it . . . until I let you drop without a parachute."

137

"You mean *this* parachute?" Jo replied, yanking the cord that dangled from his pack.

Bellowing and cursing, Ewan disappeared under a sea of white nylon.

Jo struggled to her feet and lunged for the side door.

She fought to unlatch it. Growling, she yanked on the handle as hard as she could. It barely budged. Adrenaline coursed through her veins like hot lava, making every movement seem as if it were in slow motion.

Ewan's hands clamped around her ankles. He jerked his arms back, trying to bring her down.

"You're not going anywhere!" he cried.

"Is that what you told Anka Perdova?" she yelled back. She kicked his head as hard as she could, feeling a gratifying impact.

He groaned and loosened his grip.

With her last ounces of desperate strength Jo wrenched the door handle one final time and slammed all her weight against it.

It gave way.

The handle was torn from her grasp as a rock-solid wall of wind slammed her face. The air was sucked from her lungs. Her body was lifted in the air. Her stomach rolled.

Jo hurtled toward the earth at 125 miles per hour. Only one question screamed through her brain.

If the parachute in Ewan's pack opened . . .

. . . did that mean the one in hers *wouldn't?*

There was only one way to find out.

Live and Let Spy

She pulled the cord.

And screamed.

Standing a safe distance from the carousel, Theresa fought a yawn as she watched Anka go around and around and around.

It was her third ride on the thing! How much longer can she take it? Theresa wondered in exasperation.

But a few minutes later Theresa's doldrums gave way to dismay. The hairs on her neck prickled—just like they had the other night when she was being followed.

She casually turned her head, scanning the crowd suspiciously, as the carousel continued on its circular path.

She froze.

There, behind a beat-up food stand, lurked the same burly guy who had trailed her the other night. She was sure of it. Even more sure when their eyes locked.

And he shot her a leering, vicious smile.

"Uh-oh!"

Theresa hightailed it to the nearest tent. She threw some money at the attendant and plunged inside, hoping she would make it out alive.

Theresa dashed down a long hall, but she stumbled as her stomach heaved. Wha—?

The floor bubbled up and down like waves. Twisted reflections sprang up all around her, and she had to fight to keep on her feet.

Where was she?

Everywhere she looked, someone stared back at her. Tall ones, skinny ones, fat ones, deformed ones. But they all had wild brown hair and wore a long black coat. They were all *her*.

Of course! She was in the House of Mirrors!

Theresa glanced over her shoulder and gasped.

The burly guy! He was coming after her!

Theresa darted to the right and tripped over her clunky shoes. She quickly regained her balance.

After going through a few nauseating mirror rooms and hallways she was completely disoriented. She dodged other patrons, whirling at every movement she saw from the corner of her eye.

Was that him? she wondered, gasping. Her heart caught in her throat when she glimpsed a bald, portly reflection to her immediate left.

No—just a guy with his kid.

She had to keep moving.

She slipped into the next room. Rotating mirrors spun all around her. Her face appeared, disappeared, was fat, was thin, was monstrously distorted.

"I think I'm going to puke," she mumbled.

But her nausea left immediately when she spotted her burly stalker—over her shoulder in a mirror! He was only a few feet away!

His gaze locked with hers once again.

He stepped forward, smiling demoniacally. Theresa noticed with a turn of her stomach that one of his front teeth was gold.

Move it!

140

Live and Let Spy

She slipped between two spinning mirrors and through a black curtain.

Bad move. The room was pitch black!

Theresa cringed as someone grabbed her hand and forced it into what felt like a bowl of warm, wet grapes. A deep, menacing voice barked at her in Czech.

Of course, even without knowing a word of the language, Theresa knew *exactly* what the voice was saying: "Feel the eyeballs!" She'd played that game in about a hundred haunted houses back in Arizona.

How refreshing to know some cultural trends were the same all over the world.

Theresa yanked her hand away and lunged forward, bumping the table and spilling the bowl of grapes.

The voice barked angrily. A complaint, she was sure.

"Sorry," Theresa cried out to the dark. She tossed a few bills in the air. "Here. Buy yourself some fresh eyeballs."

She kept on moving forward, not sure where she was going.

A flash of light came from behind her. She turned to see the burly guy's silhouette entering through the curtain. Then all was dark again.

Time to go!

Theresa fumbled into another curtain wall on the far side of the room. But there was no seam to slip through.

A scuffle erupted behind her. Her stalker and that

feisty eyeball guy—she was sure of it. Theresa heard someone land hard on the ground with an "Oof!"

She had to find a way out fast.

Well, if she didn't have a seam, she'd have to make one!

She slipped her tiny penknife out of her pocket and slipped it into the black curtain material, sawing downward.

A beam of light sliced through.

She ripped the thick cloth apart and stuck her leg out.

Eyeball Man began shouting up a storm. At some point she was sure she hear a word that sounded like *police.*

"Yeah! Call 'em!" Theresa replied as she dove through the hole. "I could use some backup here!"

She landed with a thud outside the eyeball chamber, flat on the ground. She tried to get up, but her left foot was snagged in the black fabric. No—a hand! A massive hand had clamped down on her ankle with an iron grip!

She knew her stalker was hiding behind that black curtain. And she instantly knew he was as low to the ground as she since he had ahold of her ankle.

Instinctively she coiled up her body and drew her right knee toward her chest. With all her might she kicked out toward the moving bump in the black curtain—the stalker's head.

She felt a chunky impact through her boot.

She heard a grunt.

Her ankle was free!

Live and Let Spy

Theresa yanked her foot back, stood up, and sprinted around another corner, seeing more mirrors, more mirrors . . . and a sign for the exit!

She bolted for it full tilt. But as she rounded the corner just before the exit flap a huge, burly man blocked her way!

Her heart skipped a beat. How could he have gotten in front of her? Impossible!

The big man slowly turned around. Theresa took a step backward—then paused.

She saw a red nose. Huge painted lips. A white face. Frizzy hair.

A clown!

Theresa shuddered.

The clown leaned forward and offered the purple carnation pinned to the lapel of his green leisure suit.

She smiled. "Oh no. I'm not gonna fall for—"

Before she could finish, the carnation squirted her in the face with sugar water.

"Har-de-har-har-har!" the clown bellowed. He wasn't laughing, though. He was actually *saying* "Har, de, har, har, har!"

Theresa licked her lips, lifted her boot, and slammed it down hard on the clown's oversize right shoe.

"Ow-ooo-ow-ow-ow!" the clown cried. He jumped up and down in a circle.

"Later, Bozo." Theresa dodged the clown, pushed the exit flap aside, and ran for her life toward the nearest tram.

*   *   *

Jo screamed at the top of her lungs. Something yanked her whole body, hard.

Her free fall was broken.

A loud flapping sound filled the air. She looked up in fear.

Her parachute had opened.

"Thankyouthankyouthankyouthankyou," she chanted frantically.

Jo felt herself soaring high in the sky. Her stomach lurched, and she felt as if she were choking on her heart.

What a rush!

Then she was dangling in the air, three thousand feet above the ground. She was frozen, with nothing to do but float. Another look up and around confirmed that InterCorp's jet was out of sight.

For a moment she felt completely free and at peace, as if she were a bird in flight.

Then Jo looked down.

All she saw were trees. A huge, endless sea of trees.

Her stomach instantly did somersaults. A hundred things could happen when a person parachuted into a tree. Deep cuts. Broken limbs—and not the ones with leaves. Brutal, unsanitary body piercings. Anything. Jo felt physically sick.

Stay calm. Just breathe, she told herself.

Once she had descended enough to see the trees for the forest, her panic subsided a bit. There were a few clearings down there. All she needed to do was steer her way over to one. As she tugged at her directional cords Jo gritted her teeth and crossed her fingers.

Live and Let Spy

As she got closer and closer to the ground she realized with dread that hitting a tree was virtually unavoidable. She also realized that floating in the air was an illusion. As she neared the ground she knew she was *falling,* and parachute or not, it was still going to hurt. There was nothing to do but brace herself and hope for the best.

Suddenly leaves were whipping her face. Branches snapped all around her. Something tore into her left arm. Her body slammed into a tree trunk. Her body scraped against its ragged bark. The ground rocketed toward her.

But then she just stopped. She dangled.

Wha—?

Jo opened her eyes. The chute had snagged in the branches above her. She was stuck. The ground was about twelve feet below.

"Great," she muttered, wincing as she touched her torn left sleeve. She was bleeding, but not badly. She shook the straps of the chute, trying to dislodge herself. But no dice. There was only one way down: the hard way.

Jo slowly reached up to the chute clamps and prepared to unhook them. She took a deep breath. Maybe if she was careful—

Snap!

"Whoooaaa!"

Thud!

"Ow!"

Jo rolled to her side and coughed. The ground was frozen, and she felt as if her insides had been

145

pureed. She lay there, her cheek pressed to the ground.

"Earth to Jo," she whispered.

She shakily attempted to move her appendages. Everything seemed to work.

"I'm going to feel this in the morning," she groaned. She stared at the gash on her left arm and grimaced. "So much for that little sleeveless number I was going to wear to the pact signing."

She scanned her surroundings. Nothing but woods.

"If I even *make* it to the signing," she added.

She looked at her watch. It was 2:30 P.M. The winter sun was beginning to descend toward the horizon. That was west. Jo remembered Ewan mentioning something about the pilot heading north of the airport.

That meant she wanted to go south. If she walked long enough, she had to hit *something* . . . right?

All she could do was brush herself off, take a deep breath, and walk.

The sun was getting ready to set when Jo began to worry. She'd walked for over two hours and still saw nothing but trees. She had to have gone at least six miles. She was exhausted. And she knew if she got stuck out all night in this cold weather, she might not make it.

But just when she was about to give up hope, she heard something. A low rumble, getting louder. She took a few tentative steps forward, listening.

The rumble grew louder. Became a roar—as if something huge was coming.

Suddenly a tractor-trailer roared by, not twenty feet in front of her!

Jo gasped. A road! She plunged forward and broke through the trees. Indeed, two lanes of black-top stretched to the left and the right as far as she could see.

And a pickup truck was approaching.

"I guess this means they're on to us," Caylin said as she swiftly and efficiently dressed the many scrapes and scratches covering Jo's arms and legs.

"You think?" Jo replied bitterly.

The Spy Girls were back safe in flat 3-S that evening. They gorged on comfort food as a reward for their tough day while making a report to Uncle Sam at the same time.

"We're glad you're okay, Jo," Theresa said, her concern genuine.

"*Okay? You* try falling out of an airplane, landing in a tree, *and* hitching a three-hour ride in the back of a pickup truck in the freezing cold!"

"All right, ladies," Uncle Sam cut in. "You're alive, and we've still got a mission to accomplish. Jo, are you with us?"

Jo nodded.

"Good. The call Ewan received on the plane was from the imposter, who most likely told him she was being followed. Somehow they had figured out that you and Theresa live together."

"Right," Theresa chimed in, "and the guy chasing me was obviously one of Fake Anka's flunkies as well."

"You need to watch your backs," Uncle Sam warned. "In fact, I'm considering aborting the entire mission."

"Whoa, you can't do that!" Caylin pleaded. "We've come way too far already!"

"We can't let them get away with this," Jo said, fire burning in her eyes.

Uncle Sam sighed. "I hear you, girls. The truth is, aborting at this stage would trigger a chain reaction at InterCorp," he admitted. "The conspirators might close up shop. Right now they think they have you on the run. For this reason, I'm going to let you continue."

"All right!" Theresa cheered.

"We'll figure out something by tomorrow night," Jo promised. "We just *have* to."

aylin headed out for the theater before seven on Sunday morning. It was going to be a long day, and she wanted to be around the assassination site as much as possible. Maybe she'd spot something important. Maybe she'd get a chance to search for the real Anka. Anything.

She was prepared for the place to be a zoo, but when she entered the theater office, she was surprised to find she was the first one there.

"Lazy bums," she muttered. She figured at the very least that Ottla would be there, making sure all the preparations were, well, *prepared.*

"Oh, well," she mused. "Maybe this Spy Girl can snoop around a bit more—"

A floorboard creaked behind her. Caylin's eyes went wide. Someone was—

A gloved hand covered her mouth and the sharp barrel of an automatic pistol was jammed against her temple.

"Move and die," a low voice growled in her ear.

Oh no.

Caylin's heart leaped. Her stomach shrank. She

sighed, closed her eyes, and prepared herself for whatever would come next.

"I can't believe we have to work on a Sunday," Hannah moaned. Her hair was disheveled, and she looked half asleep.

"They want the joint to look tip-top, I guess," Theresa replied, eyes darting around. She had too many people to keep tabs on: Caylin, who had left the flat early that morning but didn't seem to be there; Fake Anka, who hadn't arrived yet; and the burly guy with the creepy gold tooth.

If either Fake Anka or Gold Tooth saw her, the jig was up.

And while most of the other dancers were milling about, Theresa could only wonder about Fake Anka. Was she at ballet practice . . . or *target* practice?

"No way Ewan will be able to recognize me now!" Jo said to her disguised reflection in the mirror.

She had given herself a total makeover, complete with a corn silk blond wig, pale skin, blue contact lenses, and red lipstick. She completed the ensemble with a stunning black evening gown— with sleeves, to cover her cuts and bruises. The finished product looked nothing like the Jo—ahem, *Selma* that Ewan Gallagher knew.

"Simplicity is the key," she told her reflection. "I could grace five covers in one month with this look!" She blew a kiss at the mirror. "Too bad I can't have a hunky underwear model on my arm. Going solo can be *such* a blow to the ego."

Once she was dressed, Jo again checked out her look in the mirror. It was so different from her usual image. The blue contacts looked so unnaturally natural to her, it was almost creepy.

But Ewan would never recognize her.

"Get ready, Mr. Gallagher," she purred to her reflection. "You're about to see the dead come back to life—and you won't even know it . . . until it's too late!"

"Where could Caylin be?" Theresa muttered under her breath. She smoothed out her deep blue velvet dress and checked her watch for the umpteenth time.

She and Caylin had arranged to meet in front of the costume closet at 5:00 P.M. But it was now almost 5:30, and there was still no sign of her. She hadn't even answered any of her beeps.

With the ballet less than two hours away, the theater was an absolute zoo. There was a chance Caylin had gotten tied up, Theresa supposed, but it was unlike her not to call or beep.

Something must have happened. Hot, unwanted tears burned behind Theresa's eyes as she imagined just how horrifying that "something" could be.

With Ewan and Fake Anka on the loose, no one was really safe. And after Ewan's attempt on Jo's life, nothing was impossible.

Theresa blinked back tears, sniffled, and made

her way to the theater office. Ottla was there in her gown, applying some makeup.

"Excuse me, Ottla? Have you seen . . . er, Muriel?" Theresa asked.

"She still hasn't reported for duty today," Ottla growled. "Of all days! Are you a friend of hers?"

"No," she lied. "I just wanted to tell her I found a book of hers backstage."

"Whatever," Ottla said angrily. "If you see her first, please tell her to find me immediately."

Now I'm *really* freaked, Theresa thought as she left the office. She ducked into a hallway to call the flat.

No answer.

Maybe Caylin went straight to the preballet reception, Theresa hoped. But deep down she doubted it.

"She's probably chatting with Jo right now, wondering where I am," she whispered. "Please . . . please let her be there."

She dashed to the upper ballroom but saw no one after two exhausting laps. Panic gripped her.

Where *is* everybody? she cried to herself, desperate to find a familiar Spy Girl face in the crowd.

Someone bumped Theresa hard.

"Excuse me," a stunning blond said in a thick French accent.

"No problem," Theresa muttered. But a few paces later she paused. That dress . . . it was one of her mother's creations! The same dress she had loaned to Jo that morning.

Theresa stared hard at the blond woman. No. It couldn't be.

But when the blond glared straight at her with a big smirk on her face, Theresa couldn't help smiling with relief.

"Gotcha!" Jo crowed, cracking up.

Theresa pulled Jo close. "Look—no kidding around, Jo. Something's wrong. *Really* wrong."

Jo's giggles instantly ceased. "What?"

"It's Caylin," Theresa replied. "She's missing."

"What?" Her fake blue eyes widened in terror. "How?"

"I don't know," Theresa said. "Let's go over to the hors d'oeuvres table and try to blend. Who knows who's watching us now."

A few minutes later Jo lined up toast points on a silver tray while Theresa stirred a large vat of caviar with a mother-of-pearl spoon.

"How come when the best food is around, I don't feel like eating it?" Jo said morosely. "Caviar, the best champagne . . . talk about class."

"No one Caylin works with has seen her," Theresa went on, ignoring Jo's food fetish. "What could have happened?"

"Have you seen Ewan or Fake Anka?"

"No."

A toast point crumbled in Jo's hand as she shuddered. "I can't touch this stuff, I'm so nervous," she whispered.

Before Theresa had a chance to respond, Julius

approached. His tuxedo was a far classier cry from the clunky boots and paint-stained clothes that she'd come to know.

"Tiffany! Thank goodness you're here," he said haughtily. "We need one bottle of merlot. Chop-chop."

Theresa's jaw muscles pulsed angrily. What a time to play fetch!

"Sure," she replied calmly. "Where?"

"Wine cellar," Julius said.

Theresa nearly dropped her spoon. She glimpsed Jo's fake blue eyes widening—she'd caught it, too!

"Wine cellar?"

"Left after props closet, down the hall, last door on the right. Go! Go!" he ordered, shooing her away.

As Theresa headed toward the exit Jo fell in step next to her.

"This place has a *wine* cellar?" Jo whispered. "Have you seen it?"

"No. I didn't even know about it. Are you thinking what I'm thinking?"

"Well, I'm thinking that the *real* Anka—"

"Reminded her folks that she's not one to *whine*," Theresa finished. "And those red splatters in the corner . . ."

The girls stared at each other.

"This is it, T.," Jo said. "I can feel it! Come on!"

154

Left after props closet," Jo whispered, making a sharp louie.

"Down the hall," Theresa continued. They gleefully barreled down at top speed.

"Last door on right," Jo said.

Sure enough, they came face-to-face with an unmarked door.

"I always thought this was a dressing room," Theresa said. She grabbed the knob. It wouldn't budge. "Locked."

"Please tell me you have—"

"The magic key," Theresa finished, dangling the key ring from her fingers. Thank goodness she'd remembered to throw it in her evening bag. She fit the key in the lock, and with a turn of the knob they found themselves in what looked like a standard office, only the lighting was considerably dimmer. Its only distinguishable design element was a long, narrow hall that branched off from the far corner of the right wall.

"Down the hall. Chop-chop," Jo mimicked.

"Don't make fun of Julius," Theresa said. "If he hadn't commanded me to fetch that stupid bottle of merlot, we wouldn't *be* here right now."

Theresa motored down the hall. When she reached the end of the passage, she turned right—*right* into Ewan!

Theresa and Jo collectively gaped in amazement.

"Watch it, you idiot!" Ewan barked, stepping back and brushing off his designer tux. "What are you doing back here?"

"Allow *me* to explain," Jo said, stepping forward with her French femme fatale accent. "I was asked to help this stagehand select the best bottle of merlot in the house for Prime Minister Karkovic." She leaned in closer to Ewan and whispered, "This poor ignorant girl has no idea what good wine is, *n'est c'est pas?* Without my help she'd happily pour vinegar for the PM and call it a day."

Theresa blinked at Jo but remained deadpan.

Ewan raised his brows, but he didn't seem to recognize either of them in the dim light. A good sign.

"Don't worry," Jo said with a wink. "The peasant doesn't speak a word of English, either."

"*I'll* get the wine for you," Ewan grumbled, holding up a hand.

As he headed to the entryway of the cellar stairs Jo and Theresa followed.

"No," he blurted. "You wait here." He started down the stairs.

Once Ewan was safely out of earshot, Theresa swatted Jo on the head. "Peasant?"

Live and Let Spy

"Hey, watch the wig!" Jo whispered indignantly. "So what's the plan here?"

"Think about it," Theresa said grimly. "There's only one thing we can do."

Jo nodded. She knew exactly what Theresa was thinking.

"Should you do the honors or I?" Theresa asked. Her hands trembled, and Jo could see the fear in her eyes.

Jo smiled. "It would be my pleasure, T."

She heard faint footsteps seconds later. This was it!

"Here's a merlot fit for a king, literally," Ewan said as he headed up the stairs. He reached the landing. "See? A very good year."

"Wonderful," Jo purred as he handed her the bottle. She gazed lovingly at the label. "Very nice." She hefted the bottle up and down in her hand, feeling its weight. "Mmm. And so *heavy*, too."

Ewan's icicle blue eyes widened in puzzlement. "Wha—?"

"Good night." Jo raised the bottle and slammed it down on Ewan's head as hard as she could.

Red wine and glass sprayed everywhere. Ewan's head snapped back and he hit the ground with a thud. His face was covered with wine and bits of glass. Small trickles of blood rolled down his cheek.

"Whoa," Theresa breathed.

"Hope it was as good for you as it was for me, Ewan," Jo muttered, brushing some glass off her pumps. "Hmmm. Lucky my dress is black."

The lights flashed three times fast. "The ballet's

starting," Theresa piped. "We don't have much time!"

They stepped over Ewan and headed down the stairs.

"This place is a maze," Jo whispered as they spun through the catacombs. "It's all dead ends. And who drinks this much wine?"

"Come on, this way," Theresa said. She pulled at Jo's arm.

"Anka!" Jo called out into the stale air.

"Caylin!" Theresa shouted.

Over and over again they kept calling. No answers came.

"Don't give up yet," Theresa told Jo as she continued to go up and down each and every aisle. A few minutes later Jo saw Theresa abruptly stop short.

"Wait," she said, perking up her ears. "Do you hear something?"

Jo stopped to listen. "Not a thing."

"Maybe it was just my imagination." Theresa shrugged and continued on.

After a few more minutes passed, Theresa halted again. "I definitely heard something that time," she proclaimed.

"What'd it sound like?" Jo asked.

"A cry of some sort," Theresa replied. "Over there, I think. By those magnum bottles."

Then Jo heard it. A muffled cry from deep behind a wall of bottles. They both moved closer and peered between the magnums.

"Look!" Jo cried, reaching between two bottles

158

and feeling the wall behind them. "It's wood! A door!"

"Hello?" Theresa called.

The cries came again, louder this time.

"That's it!" Jo exclaimed. "We have to get through that door."

"Check out the floor," Theresa ordered. "There are wheel marks. The wine rack is on wheels! Grab an end."

They slowly rolled the massive rack of bottles to the side. The wheels creaked and moaned, but they moved. And sure enough, they had uncovered a stout wooden door.

"That thing must be a thousand years old," Jo surmised.

"Maybe," Theresa replied, fishing the magic key ring out once again. "But the lock is brand-new."

Theresa slid the key into the lock with a smile and turned. It didn't budge.

"Uh-oh," she said.

"What?" Jo asked.

Theresa jiggled the key. "Take a guess."

"Aw, no fair!" Jo cried. "It worked on all the other ones!"

"Not *this* one." Theresa slipped the key back in her purse and sighed. "Now what?"

"Well . . . ," Jo began.

"You have something?" Theresa asked.

Jo wiped her wine-stained hands on her designer dress and yanked a bobby pin from her hair. "What do you think?"

"I think we're doomed," Theresa replied glumly.

"It can't hurt to try," Jo replied sharply. She inserted the bobby pin in the lock and tried to jimmy it. "This always works in the movies."

"Jo, that's a state-of-the-art lock," Theresa lectured. "It has a complex series of tumblers that will only open to a specific computer-coded key. Not magic keys, and certainly not bobby—"

The pin clicked and turned in the keyhole.

Jo giggled and beamed up at Theresa, whose jaw was practically on the floor.

"I'll accept your apology later, Brainiac," Jo said. She turned the knob and pulled the door open with a loud, grating squeal.

"Hello?" Theresa called. "Caylin? Anka?"

They peered into the dim chamber—then gasped. Both Anka and Caylin were sardined in the tiny crawl space, their arms and legs bound.

"You're okay!" Theresa wailed, tears of relief falling down her face.

"Ohmigosh!" Jo cried. She crouched down and hastily untied the ropes that bound them.

Theresa pulled Anka out, then Caylin. Both young women were sobbing. Caylin's burgundy formal was covered with a film of dust and grime.

"It's about time," Caylin complained through her tears.

"You're free now." Theresa wrapped Caylin in a hug. "I was so afraid you'd—"

"Not so fast!"

"Ewan!" Jo cried.

Theresa whipped around. Ewan stood behind

160

them, sneering as blood and wine dripped off his chiseled features. "Nobody's going anywhere!"

"And who's going to stop us?" Caylin growled, massaging blood back into her fists.

"Who do you think?" Ewan pulled an automatic pistol from his coat pocket.

"You shouldn't play with guns, Ewan," Jo warned in her Selma voice. "People could get hurt."

Ewan's eyes went wide. "Y-You!" he sputtered. He actually smiled through the blood. "Skydiving suits you, Selma. The impact did you some good. I prefer blonds."

"I think you've had too much wine." Jo pulled the wig off and tossed it aside. "I like myself just the way I am, thank you."

"I liked you, too, Selma," Ewan replied. He picked a shard of glass out of his cheek and regarded it momentarily before tossing it aside. "That's why I'll have to kill you first."

Ewan leveled the gun on Jo.

"Hey, lover boy," Theresa called out.

Ewan glanced at her and sneered. "Yeah?"

"If you're gonna take her out, don't forget the keys to the car!"

Theresa tossed the magic key ring at Ewan. He reached out with his free hand and casually caught them.

He stared at the key ring and smiled. "What, no convertible?"

Theresa smiled. "I *knew* I forgot something!" She snapped her fingers for emphasis.

A blinding spark shot up from Ewan's fist. His face froze in shock and his whole body stiffened, quaking. The gun dropped from his other hand.

In a few seconds the stun gun shut down. Ewan hovered there for a moment, wobbling, fist frozen around the key ring. Then he collapsed in a heap.

"on't forget the keys to the car'?" Jo echoed, beaming. "Jeez, T., you couldn't come up with anything better than *that?*"

"Worked pretty well, I'd say," Theresa said matter-of-factly.

Caylin stepped forward and snatched up Ewan's pistol. "No more socializing," she commanded, tossing the rope Jo's way. "Help me tie this creep up. We don't have much time!"

"Okay," Jo said. "T., you take Anka upstairs. While we tie Ewan up, I'll search him for his key chain. Let's lock him up in that crawl space and give him a taste of his own medicine."

While Jo helped Caylin tie up Ewan, Theresa helped Anka run upstairs. They headed straight for the costume closet.

"Why are you taking me here?" Anka asked frantically as she swabbed at her dirty hands and face with baby wipes. "You're with Caylin, yes?"

"Yes, but I don't have time to explain—"

"Caylin already did," Anka said. "I know all about my look-alike."

"Then you have to change fast!" Theresa

told her. "You have to go onstage and dance!"

"I don't know if I can," Anka replied. "The ropes cut into me because they were so tight. My feet are tingling too much."

They reached the costume closet. Theresa opened the door and shoved her inside. "Please, Anka . . . you have to try."

Anka stared at her a moment, then nodded. "I will. The audience out there deserves it . . . and so do I." She began shedding her dirty clothes. "I don't understand. How can someone look like me and dance like me?"

"This imposter—she had plastic surgery or something. Who knows, but everyone thinks she's you. When the lights go out for intermission, we're pretty sure she's going to shoot Gogol Karkovic from the stage."

"Caylin told me all that, too," Anka said as she cleaned her arms and legs. "It's *got* to be the craziest thing I've ever heard."

"I know it sounds like a bad episode of *The Twilight Zone*, but it's dead serious."

Anka struggled into her bodysuit. "Ewan kept saying I was going to kill Karkovic, but I couldn't understand how or why," she explained. "I thought it was because someone had found out my secret— that I faked being from Russia to get into the NRB. But what does that have to do with Karkovic? He's a good guy with a big heart. Why in the world would anyone want to kill him?"

"Because he's a good guy with a big heart,

that's why." Theresa shook her head. "Oh, man, you must have been going crazy in there coming up with conspiracy theories. So why did you do it? Change your name and fake your heritage, I mean."

"Dancing is . . . well, it's the only thing I've ever been able to do right, you know? If I couldn't dance for a living, then I didn't have another reason to live." Anka scrambled to find the right-size slippers. "Ever since I was little, I wanted to dance with the NRB. And I made my dream come true. I didn't do it to hurt anybody."

Theresa cocked her head to the side as she helped Anka fasten her skirt. "Well, it's pretty dishonest, but it doesn't mean you should be framed for murder."

"Seriously." Anka arranged her hair into a tight bun. "But then before Caylin got caught, I was all alone in that little room, thinking, *I'm getting what I deserve. I should be punished for what I've done. What Ewan's doing is right.*" She securely fastened bobby pins all over her head. "I thought I was going to go crazy. I was actually *agreeing* with that psycho."

"Oh, Anka, no," Theresa said gently. "No one deserves to be treated the way you were. No one deserves to be punished like this."

Anka shakily put on her stage makeup and turned to face Theresa. "This is beyond belief. But . . . well, the show must go on, right?"

"Right." Theresa smiled. "Everything's going to be okay, Anka. No matter what happens, you have witnesses to prove you weren't the murderer." She paused. "But now if only the murder *itself* can be prevented . . ."

"It's us," Caylin called as she pounded on the closet door.

Theresa let Caylin and Jo in and turned her attention to adjusting a net around Anka's tight bun. Theresa smoothed back the last few stray, matted strands of hair, and Anka was ready to roll.

"I say our only chance is to grab Fake Anka the next time she leaves the stage and replace her with the real Anka," Caylin said quickly. "Anka, will she leave the stage before intermission?"

Anka strained to hear what music was currently playing. "One more time, in about four minutes," she replied. "She'll exit for about ten seconds, stage left."

"We'll be there," Jo vowed.

"That is, if she doesn't shoot Karkovic within the next four minutes," Theresa said gravely. "Let's go."

The Spy Girls formed a human circle around the ballerina.

"Stay back, Anka. No one can see you yet!" Caylin insisted.

They inched their way toward stage left, praying they weren't too late.

The lights dimmed seconds later.

"Oh no!" Theresa gasped.

The girls collectively held their breath as they listened for a shot, but none came.

"It's just the end of the scene," Anka whispered as they reached a darkened, secluded corner at stage left—their final destination. "She should be coming offstage in a few seconds."

The resounding music started up again.

"Here she comes!" Caylin said.

The imposter danced toward them, oblivious.

Theresa placed her hands on Anka's shoulders. "Break a leg!" she whispered.

Both Ankas' eyes widened as they faced each other for a split second. But before Fake Anka could shriek, scream, or freak, Caylin tackled her to the ground while Jo gagged her with her black silk wrap.

The real Anka entered seamlessly into the scene without so much as missing a beat. A real trouper, she was.

"Do you want to be tied up or down?" Jo asked Fake Anka, who was kicking and struggling under Caylin's grip, her eyes glittering with fury. Jo crouched next to the imposter and offered her a satisfied smile.

As she bound Fake Anka's hands Theresa noticed that the dancer seemed to be frantically struggling to lunge to the left. Theresa scanned the area—the exit, the curtains, the table. . . .

The table!

A black box had been placed on top of the table. Theresa had used that table hundreds of times; she'd never seen that box before.

"What's that?" Theresa asked sharply. "It looks like a shoe box. What's in it?"

Fake Anka growled.

"Check out that box, Cay," Jo called as she secured Fake Anka's kicking feet. "Whatever's in it, Fake Anka here wants it pretty bad."

"It's probably her gun," Caylin said as she snatched up the innocent-looking box and peeked inside. She did a double take. The box wasn't holding a gun at all.

It was holding a timer.

A *ticking* timer.

"Uh, guys?" Caylin called out.

"What?" Jo and Theresa asked in stereo.

"Does either of you know how to defuse a bomb?"

"*What?*"

Caylin held the box upright so Jo and Theresa could see the timer counting down from 3:34. "Looks like there's been a change of plans."

"Ohmigosh!" Theresa exclaimed, petrified. Jo just stared at it in horrified silence, saying everything by saying nothing at all.

"Talk to us!" Caylin cried, staring into Fake Anka's spiteful eyes. "I don't get it. It was *supposed* to be a *gun.*"

"Maybe it wasn't," Theresa said. "We never knew for sure. Maybe it was meant to happen this way all along."

A few feet away the ballet continued. The music crescendoed as the stakes both on- and offstage grew higher and higher.

The timer hit 3:00.

"There's no time," Caylin said. "We need to disarm this thing *now.*"

Theresa searched in her purse. "I need something to work with!"

Jo produced a pair of tweezers. "Try these. They're great on eyebrows."

"Ungag her," Theresa demanded. "I need her to help."

2:47.

Jo yanked the scarf from Fake Anka's mouth.

"You better tell me how to disarm this," Theresa commanded, "or we're all dead meat."

"No, not us," Fake Anka taunted them the second she was ungagged. "Just Karkovic."

2:36.

"But I have the bomb in my hands," Theresa said, confused.

"You have the timer," Fake Anka explained. "The bomb is in the wine cellar. Where von Strauss is taking Karkovic right this minute."

"What about Karkovic's bodyguards?" Theresa asked. "Won't they—"

Fake Anka shook her head. "The bodyguards know all about this secret little meeting. And they don't suspect a thing."

Without a word Caylin hefted Ewan's gun and the magic key chain and took off running.

"Be careful!" Jo called.

"Why put a bomb in the cellar?" Theresa asked, indignant. "You would have killed Karkovic and Anka, too. You'd have no one to take the rap."

"Von Strauss was going to bring her up after he took Karkovic down," Fake Anka spat. "You did half our work for us. I should thank you."

"Don't bother," Theresa snapped. "Now tell me how to disarm this thing."

"Why bother?" Fake Anka asked flippantly. "*We'll* be okay. Who cares?"

"I think *you* will," Jo angrily chimed in. "Your boyfriend's down there, too."

"I don't believe you," Fake Anka said. She stared at Jo uncertainly.

Jo glanced at the timer as it passed the two-minute mark. She reached into her purse and held up Ewan's Lamborghini-logo key chain. "I believe this is the key I used to lock him in. Do you recognize it?"

"You're lying," Fake Anka snarled, eyes darting from Jo to Theresa and back.

"You know you love him," Theresa said. "Do you want him dead?"

"Why should I believe you?" Fake Anka screeched. "Why should I?"

Jo looked deep into her eyes. "Because if you don't, your boyfriend'll be dead and *you'll* be the only one to blame."

As Caylin dashed through the rows of wine she caught a glimpse of von Strauss racing toward the exit. Behind him she could hear Karkovic screaming and pounding on the cellar door.

She gripped Ewan's gun . . . but wasn't sure if she could use it.

She had a better idea.

She stuck out a foot and caught von Strauss as he sprinted by. The big man sprawled headlong onto the concrete floor with a cry of rage. Caylin smoothly stepped out of the shadows and tossed the Tower key ring at him. He caught it and stared in confusion.

"What are you doing?" von Strauss demanded.

"Saving the world from evil," she said, snapping her fingers.

"Wha-what?" he cried as the shock disabled him and he writhed on the floor in pain.

Caylin immediately scrambled to unlock the crawl space door and set Karkovic free. But she didn't have a key. . . .

Von Strauss did!

Quickly she patted his tuxedo pockets. Left. Right. There!

She snatched his key chain from his prone form and frantically searched for the right one. "Go, go, go," she chanted. Her hands were shaking.

The fifth key worked. She hauled the door open and saw Karkovic crouched next to the bound and gagged Ewan.

"Come on, sir," Caylin ordered, waving Karkovic out. "We have to get you out of here!"

:19

"Red or black, Anka?" Theresa pleaded, tweezers poised. "Red or black?"

The music escalated to a deafening level.

:16

Jo: "Tell me, Anka."

:13

Theresa: "Ewan's going to die."

:12

Jo: "You're a murderer."

:11

Theresa: "Red or black?"

:10

Jo: "You love him—you know you do."

:09

Theresa: "Just say it, *red or black*."

With eight seconds left on the clock tears of frustration welled in Fake Anka's eyes. A single tear rolled down her cheek.

"Red," she whispered.

Praying she wasn't bluffing, Theresa closed her eyes and gripped the red wire with the tweezers.

"Do it," Jo said.

Theresa clipped the red wire. The timer's LCD display faded to black.

While Fake Anka broke into sobs, Jo and Theresa hugged each other tightly.

"You did it," Jo whispered, squeezing her hard.

"No," Theresa said, pulling back to look into Jo's fake baby blues. "*We* did it!"

As soon as I get von Strauss processed, you're both going with me," Interpol Agent Johnson told Fake Anka and Ewan as he cuffed them to separate poles in a dark backstage corner. "In the meantime, Spy Girls, they're all yours. Off the record, of course."

"Of course," Theresa repeated, smiling smugly. There were a lot of loose ends to tie up, and this was their big chance to get some answers.

"I cannot believe you two—two—women are the ones I was having followed," Fake Anka said, her English failing in her fury. She glared at Jo and Theresa.

Theresa glared right back. "How'd you even know to have us trailed in the first place?"

"The computer—you were fools," Fake Anka snarled. "After you break into my dressing room—you did not leave—log off—Internet," she said. "Dumb mistake. That is how I knew someone has been snooping around."

"Then she told me," Ewan said, "so I hired a private investigator."

"The big guy who followed me and left me that postcard, right?" Theresa asked.

"Yes," Fake Anka spat. "He saw you talking to the blond one, too." She motioned to Caylin. "She was first to come in today, so Ewan took her hostage. I was glad. I've always hated blonds."

Caylin narrowed her blue eyes. "You don't impress me all that much, either, thanks."

"And I guess this same investigator must have spilled the beans to you about my little gallery date with your pig boyfriend, hmmm?" Jo asked.

Fake Anka glared at Jo. Then at Ewan. Then at the floor.

"What I want to know is," Caylin asked, "why did you come up with this elaborate plan with the bomb in the cellar? Couldn't you have just shot Karkovic from the stage?"

Caylin received bizarre looks from all directions.

She cleared her throat. "Well, I didn't mean that would have been a good thing, but—"

"I wanted to shoot Karkovic," Fake Anka said. "I'm a good shot. My uncle, he teach me. I *told* Ewan, but he wouldn't listen." She jerked her head in Ewan's direction. "He said we can put Anka's fingerprints on the box and frame her in an easier way. Less people hurt, but she would still go to jail and die."

While Fake Anka described this setup, the real Anka approached. The ballet had ended to a standing ovation, and she still wore her stage costume. "But why would you get plastic surgery and pretend to be someone you're not to frame

174

someone you don't even know?" she asked incredulously. "Did you do it for Ewan?"

"Of course not," Fake Anka said scornfully, glaring right back into the real Anka's eyes. She drew herself up and threw back her shoulders. "I'm Anna Poritzkova. You beat me out for my rightful place in the New Russian Ballet four years ago, and I swore I'd get revenge." She smiled bitterly. "I almost did. And I got to dance."

Anka's jaw dropped. The Spy Girls looked at one another in disbelief.

"Sorry to interrupt here," Interpol Agent Johnson said, "but I need to ask Ms. Perdova a few questions."

As he pulled her away Caylin noticed that Anka didn't once take her eyes off Fake—er, *Anna Poritzkova.*

"And it's curtain call for these two as well," Interpol Agent Zimmerman said, uncuffing Ewan and Fake Anka from the pole and commanding them to stand with von Strauss.

"Thanks for the memories!" Jo cheered. She winked at Ewan as he was led away.

"I'll get all of you for this," von Strauss threatened. "You just wait."

"Yeah, you would've gotten away with it, too," Caylin said in mock fear. "If it wasn't for us meddling gals."

Jo smiled sweetly and hollered for Agent Johnson to hold up. "Mr. von Strauss's going-away comment reminded me: You might want to check into InterCorp's secret tax files, too," she said. "They're hidden in the third-floor supply closet."

Von Strauss's face reddened with rage. "Why, you little—"

The Spy Girls were still laughing over von Strauss's expression when Ottla approached and introduced the president of the Czech Republic.

"I'd like to thank you for all your hard work," he said, shaking each of their hands. "You have done our country a great service."

The Spy Girls couldn't help but smile at one another.

"Cool," Theresa whispered.

"Thank you again," he proclaimed. "I just don't know what to say."

The Czech leader then turned to Karkovic. "Sir, would you like us to postpone the signing in light of everything that has happened?"

Karkovic smiled and shook his head. "Everything that happened is the biggest reason of all *to* go through with it," he replied. "We cannot let evil triumph over the goodness of humanity. I want to finish what I have started. After all," he concluded, "that's what freedom is all about."

"I can't believe I'm actually bummed to be leaving somewhere so cold," Jo exclaimed over her suitcase back at 3-S. She'd grown to appreciate Prague and its quiet charm. She really was going to miss it.

Live and Let Spy

"I know what you mean," Caylin said as she folded a sweater and placed it in her suitcase. "While I'm psyched to go home, a part of me wants to stay."

"Me three," Theresa agreed with a sad smile.

At that moment the door buzzer sounded—two short, two long.

"The secret buzz!" Jo said, rushing to the door to get it. "Hope it's the same delivery dude from last time!" She smoothed her hair before she opened the door.

"Special delivery for Caylin, Jo, and Theresa," a dark-haired woman announced. She handed Jo a folded paper bag before turning on her heels.

"What could this be?" Jo wondered. She set the bag down on the dining room table so they could open it together.

"Three cappuccinos to go!" Caylin announced. She removed a trio of steaming cups from the bag.

"And that rare Pearl Jam CD!" Theresa squealed. She yanked the disc out so fast, she ripped the bag. "Now, who knew I was a total Eddie Vedder freak?"

"Looks like you're about to find out," Jo said, reaching for the folded note that had flopped out onto the table. "'Next stop: the birthplace of grunge,'" Jo recited, "'where you'll crack the code of the century—Uncle Sam.'"

"Huh?" Caylin muttered, utterly confused.

"Seattle!" Jo cheered, totally pumped.

177

"The coolest city in the universe!" Theresa chimed in.

Theresa passed coffees to Jo and Caylin and took one for herself.

"Lids off," Jo commanded, a twinkle in her eye.

They all removed their coffee cup lids.

"To our next taste of adventure," Theresa toasted.

Caylin smiled. "Ready, set, sip!"

And they did.

About the Author

Elizabeth Cage is a saucy pseudonym for a noted young adult writer. Her true identity and current whereabouts are classified.

Printed in the United States
By Bookmasters